FIGH

The slave tracker was startled when Maxwell grabbed the whip and yanked. Not since his first days as a bounty man had Papa Beaulieu met such resistance. He tried to resist the pull of the whip, but could not. So he let its handle go, forgetting it was still attached to him by the loop around his wrist. He had to do something, and fast. He reached for his single-shot flintlock pistol.

Maxwell almost fell off balance when Beaulieu let go of the whip, but then the thong on Beaulieu's wrist caught, and Maxwell began tugging again, pulling the slave hunter toward him with an unyielding pressure. He saw Beaulieu reach for his gun. . . .

Maxwell dropped his sack and jerked the knife from his rope belt. He gave one final, mighty tug, and Beaulieu stumbled forward. Just before the two men hit, Maxwell plunged his knife into the slave hunter's stomach.

Books by John Legg

Mountain Country series:
Southwest Thunder
Winter Thunder
Mountain Thunder

Buckskins and Blood
The Frontiersman
Fire Along the Big Muddy
Buckskin Vengeance
Flintlock Trail

Published by HarperPaperbacks

FLINTLOCK TRAIL

JOHN LEGG

HarperPaperbacks

A division of HarperCollinsPublishers

![HarperPaperbacks logo] **HarperPaperbacks**
A Division of HarperCollinsPublishers
10 East 53rd Street, New York, N.Y. 10022-5299

This is a work of fiction. The characters, incidents, and
dialogues are products of the author's imagination and are not to
be construed as real. Any resemblance to actual events or
persons, living or dead, is entirely coincidental.

ISBN 0-06-101064-2

HarperCollins®, ![logo] ®, and HarperPaperbacks™
are trademarks of HarperCollinsPublishers, Inc.

Cover illustration by Rick McCollum

First printing: July 1997

Printed in the United States of America

❖ 10 9 8 7 6 5 4 3 2 1

To the late Janice Holt Giles,
whose books were such an inspiration to me.
Gracious, but you were a superb writer.
My humble thanks.

FLINTLOCK TRAIL

Late Spring 1815

He was used to bustling waterfronts, whether on rivers or the ocean, so Saint Louis held no fear or surprise for Jacques Maxwell as he stepped off the keelboat.

"Zis looks like ze place for me to had a good time," Maxwell said to no one in particular.

He stood there just off the quay for a few moments, looking around. If it were not for the few nice homes up on the bluff, it could have been any of several dozen places Maxwell had cast his anchor ever so briefly.

Dirty, sweating workmen carted bales and boxes, kegs and cases filled with many of the wonders of this bounteous land to and from various kinds of boats. Voyageurs sat on wooden boxes to the side, playing cards on a wooden trunk, their games accompanied by much shouting and good-natured cursing. Muddy children ran in and out of the muck, tossing clods of the slimy earth at one another, all the while shrieking and hooting at their victims.

With the odd rolling gait of a seaman on land, which he was, Maxwell strolled down the rutted mud track that passed for a waterfront street. As he ambled along the furrowed path, he was careful to avoid the carts and wagons that rattled and clunked along, usually at a breakneck pace, heedless of whoever or whatever was in their way.

In the short journey he made while looking for a saloon, he passed three brawls, two minor fights, and three cockfights. Several knots of men were dancing a Virginia reel to the tune of a single fiddle. He waded through clots of grunting, snorting hogs, braying mules, high-spirited horses, chattering chickens, barking, snapping mongrels, and hell-raising children.

Since rancid bars frequently festooned the waterfront with their foul facades, Maxwell had no trouble finding an appropriately disreputable-looking place. He hauled himself inside and walked straight toward the bar.

The place was about what he expected, since he had a wealth of knowledge of similar sinkholes of degradation. In fact, he felt quite at home in such pits of rum and other assorted sinful pleasures.

"*Bonjour, Monsieur le* Bar man," Maxwell said pleasantly, a broad smile creasing his dark brown face. "You can gave me a bottle of rum, eh. *Tout de suite.*"

The bald, sagging-skinned bartender stared at him for a moment, then shrugged. He grabbed a bottle of rum and set it on the makeshift counter with a thud. He kept one hand firmly around the neck of the dark bottle. He held out the other hand, palm raised and open. "Rum hereabouts is hard to come by, boy. An' that means it ain't cheap. You understand." He didn't care a whit whether Maxwell did or not. "That'll be twelve dollars."

Maxwell whistled softly. "You ain't gonna lied about zhat, my frain. I guarontee. *Merde*, but I t'ink you might be fixing to stole my teeth nex' wit' zose kind of prices."

The barkeep shrugged again. "I got cheaper swill, if you ain't of a mind to pay my rate. Or you can haul your raggedy hide off to somewhere else. Don't make me no nevermind."

Maxwell smiled, but there was little humor in it. He was an easygoing man by nature, but he was by no means a pushover. He could be as tough, mean, and nasty as any man. The thing was, though, it usually took him a little time to get to that point. All he had to decide now was whether he wanted to pay the exorbitant price, get some cheaper liquor, or drift on to another sordid haven for people like him.

"You drove an 'ard bargain, *monsieur*," Maxwell said fatalistically. "But I'll take it. What ze 'ell. As long as zis was good rum."

"The finest in Saint Louis," the barkeeper said, not moving either hand.

Maxwell suddenly felt like punching the bartender in the face, knowing the man was lying. But he just shrugged, pulled some coins out of the leather pouch hanging from his belt, and dropped them on the counter, missing by a hair's breadth the bartender's outstretched hand. He did not apologize for the deliberate act.

With a snarl, the bartender unclamped his hand from the bottleneck and swept the coins up into his other hand.

Trying to hide a devilish smile, Maxwell waited until the bar man had turned and taken two steps before he said, "Ah, *monsieur, un verre, s'il vous plait.* A glass, please."

The bartender was livid as he turned, grabbed a tall, dirty glass, and slammed it onto the planking that served as the bar.

"*Merci,*" Maxwell said with an ingratiating grin. "Now you may gone about your business."

"Bah!" the bartender muttered as he grumbled his way off.

Maxwell filled his large glass to the brim and, in one long swallow, downed its contents. Smacking his lips at the familiar sweet taste, he refilled the glass. It was far from the best rum he'd ever had, but it was good enough, and it had been a little while since he'd had any at all.

Glass in hand, Maxwell turned and leaned his elbows behind him on the improvised bar, then looked around the dismal place. The saloon was filled with the usual collection of boatmen, roustabouts, voyageurs, laborers, and fur trappers generally found in such low dives. There was a smattering of slightly higher-class men, mostly small-time traders and poor merchants, Maxwell figured.

Maxwell sipped his rum, watching the saloon's activities with little interest. A few slovenly, third-rate prostitutes wearily tried to ply their trade around the room, with a fair amount of success. The male patrons were not very discerning in such matters. Maxwell wasn't all that discriminating about these things either, but at the moment he was not in the market for a fast roll on a lice-infested tick mattress with one of these rank, unkempt women.

Other men gambled on cards or checkers. A fiddler stood forlornly in a corner, playing melancholy tunes that hinted at Ireland and France and Spain. Some men just talked, often with bursts of loudness punctuated with curses, shouts of glee, or laughter.

Maxwell set his glass on the wood plank and pulled out a long, thin, clay pipe. He filled it and then lit it with a burning candle he plucked from its wax base on the bar. He wondered what he would do now. He was not one for doing nothing. He craved action and activity. But he had precious few real skills, or at least ones that he could use to find a reasonable job. He could handle himself with a pistol or cutlass, or even his fists, and he had killed more than once in battles he had been in, but those things were not likely to find him decent employment here in Saint Louis.

He wasn't even sure why he had come to Saint Louis in the first place, other than that he had grown tired of waterfront cities around New Orleans and southwest along the Gulf of Mexico. There were other, more personal reasons why he wanted to get away from his old haunts, but they still did not explain why he had headed up the Mississippi River to Saint Louis. About the only thing he could think of was that Saint Louis already had a reputation as a lively town, with plenty of activity to keep even the most jaded of men occupied for some time.

He sighed. There was no reason to make any decisions right now. He had just pulled into the city, and he had enough money to keep him going for at least a little while—if he refrained from buying many more twelve-dollar bottles of rum. He had to smile at that, but with a touch of sourness. He hated to be taken like he had been. On the other hand, he almost admired the bartender for being brazen enough to do it. It was of little matter now. However, it did give him an idea.

Maxwell finally jammed the cork back into the bottle, lifted the bottle in one hand, and sauntered out of the foul saloon. He wandered around for a while, taking in the sights, sounds, and smells of Saint Louis. After an hour or so, he began to feel comfortable about the place. Not that he had felt uncomfortable so far, it was just that he was in a new place and therefore unaccustomed to it. But it didn't take long to realize that there wasn't much different here from anywhere else he had been. He heard plenty of French and Spanish being spoken, and he saw no difference in the rough men who prowled Saint Louis's streets from those who strutted around New Orleans or Galveston Island or any other place he had been.

He soon found himself a place to stay. For his money, he got a bed in a long room crammed with poor beds with dirty tick mattresses, and two almost edible meals a day. The cost wasn't too outrageous, though on his first night there he began to think that perhaps he had been taken again. The chorus of burps, snores, farts, grunts, and other assorted noises—with the accompanying clouds of noxious fumes—as well as the stench of unwashed bodies, stale whiskey, urine, and more—made the place nearly unfit for human habitation.

Over the next few days, Maxwell sampled the wares and the atmosphere in a number of the other fetid saloons scattered like bird droppings along the Mississippi River's waterfront. None was any worse than the first one he had entered—the Hog's Blood. Of course, none was any better either. In a spasm of perversity, Maxwell decided that the Hog's Blood would be his retreat of choice.

He entered the Hog's Blood and headed straight for the bar, only to encounter the same fractious bartender as before. Maxwell smiled ingratiatingly. "Now, I t'ink we got off to a poor start ze last time I was 'ere. And maybe zat was my fault. No matter, though. *Mais non*. But after some deep t'inking, I believe zis place was ze pick of ze litter, *n'est-ce pas?* So why don' we was trying again to be frains, eh?"

"Listen to me, you piss-reekin' black Frog," the bartender snarled, "I don't give a good goddamn what you want. I ain't about to be friends with the likes of you, and you pay whatever the hell I say you'll pay. You got that, Frog boy?"

There were few things in life that would set Maxwell off right away. One of them was making fun of his ancestry. He was the illegitimate son of a Louisiana plantation-owning, slave-holding father, and a half-Cajun, half-Creole slave, which made him one-quarter black, which showed in his brown skin and full lips. His parentage also made him a French speaker from both sides of his mother's parents. While he spoke English quite well, though admittedly with a grandiloquent Cajun lilt, he had learned French at the same time.

So when this idiot bartender disparaged both the French and black portions of his ancestry, Maxwell saw red. "Zose weren't nice t'ings to said to me, *tu fumier*—you shit," he muttered. With that, he suddenly thumped the bartender in the forehead with the side of a fist.

The barkeep staggered back a step or two before regaining his footing. But by then, Maxwell had rolled over the wood planks and was on his feet in front of his foe. He popped the man twice more in the face, rather enjoying himself.

But the barkeep was not about to put up with this nonsense for long. Maxwell's punches had done little to hurt him; the first one had simply taken him by surprise. He wiped a hand across his face and looked down at it to see blood from his nose and split lip. With a grimace, he stepped up and launched a hard fist at Maxwell.

The mixed-blood was taken by surprise this time, and he cursed himself as he went down when the bartender's fist cracked against his cheek. He had been too confident, too cocky. It was not the way to come out of such fights alive. As he scrambled up, shaking the wooziness out of his head, he vowed not to be caught unawares again.

At about five-foot-nine and one hundred seventy pounds, Maxwell was considerably smaller than the bartender, but he could tell already that he was almost as strong, and had more speed. Trying to regain his full senses, Maxwell danced back and forth, just out of reach of the bartender's roundhouse punches. When his head cleared, Maxwell suddenly took two steps backward, then ran forward and jumped. His feet crashed into the barkeep's chest, driving him back and down.

Before the barkeep really knew what was going on, Maxwell was on his chest and had the tip of a long, thin dagger gently caressing the underside of the man's jaw.

"Now, *monsieur*, maybe you was to t'ink again before you say zem ugly t'ings about me, a man who tried only to be your *ami*. *Ça va?* Did you t'ink you can do zat, eh?"

"Piss on you, Froggie," the bartender gargled, uncowed and still angry.

"You don't seem to learn very well, *monsieur*." Maxwell pushed the knife a little, until the sharp tip broke the bartender's skin, releasing a small trickle of blood. "Maybe you wan' to ret'ought your t'inking," Maxwell said softly.

Before the barkeep could say anything, Maxwell heard a voice from behind him say, "Let him up." The voice held command and authority.

Maxwell glanced over his shoulder and saw a medium-sized, paunchy man dressed in a manner he thought fashionable but was really just a slightly better grade of shabbiness than everyone else around here wore. "And why should I done zat, *monsieur?*" he asked.

"Because Ah'm the owner of this heah place,

and Ah'd rather not have my bartender's blood all ovah the floor."

"Dat don't sounded like no good reason to me," Maxwell allowed.

The owner shrugged. "Ah also have a pistol and can blow your damned brains out right here and now, if you'd rather."

Maxwell noticed the heavy flintlock pistol in the man's waistband. He grinned a little. "Ah, now zat is a good reason to done what you say, *monsieur*." He pulled the dagger away from the bartender's neck, and rose, sliding the knife away into the top of one tall boot.

The bartender stood, too, though he had a sneer on his face. He figured that with his boss here, he would have the pleasure of throwing this troublesome bastard out into the muddy street.

"Get out, Hathaway," the owner said to the barkeep.

"What?" Hathaway asked, shocked.

"You heard me, goddammit. Get out."

"But why, Mister Womack?"

"Because you're an idiot and a smart-mouthed one besides. Ah got no mo' use for you."

The choler rose in Hathaway's face, and he looked as if he was about to attack Womack, but he decided against it. "If that's the way you want it, damn you, fine. I'll just collect my pay and be gone."

"What pay?" Womack asked, feigning innocence. "With what you consumed behind the bar, you've been more than adequately compensated, Hathaway. Goodbye."

A furious Hathaway stomped out.

"I t'ink zat was a foolish t'ing, *monsieur*," Maxwell said.

"Are you afraid of him?"

"Of zat fool? Hah! I am more of afraid of *mon vieille mémé*—my old granny," Maxwell spat out.

"Then don't concern yourself with Mister Hathaway. He won't bother anyone." Womack paused, then asked, "Would you like a job as my bartender?"

Maxwell thought it over for perhaps five seconds, then shrugged. He needed a job to pay his way, and this one would do for the time being. He nodded. "*Oui.*"

Within a month of taking the job as a bartender at the Hog's Blood saloon, Maxwell was bored. Sure, there were plenty of fights to break up or force outside, bullheaded drunks to settle down and get rid of, and enough business to keep him relatively busy. Still, he was used to more intensive, dangerous activity. Life as a bartender and bouncer quickly paled, but he could figure out nothing else to do with himself, so he began to contemplate pulling up stakes and moving on again. He had only to make the decision as to where.

One of the benefits of his position was that he met men from all over, and each would bring tales of different places—the giant lakes to the north and northeast; big rivers east of Saint Louis; the grand Missouri River, which flowed into the Mississippi River a bit north of Saint Louis; flat, apparently barren lands teeming with buffalo to the west. He even heard a few talk of lofty, menacing mountains that roared contemptuously up out of the plains far to the west. It gave

Maxwell plenty to think about, an abundance of choices to pick from.

As a result, he lingered on, despite the boredom. He was in no real hurry to get anywhere. And he did enjoy his job. He liked meeting the varied people, hearing the disparate stories—most of which he was certain were hellacious exaggerations, if not outright lies—and ruling his little domain here.

Still, he longed for some adventure. He had had a lot of it in his twenty-two years, but that only made him crave more. He used to wonder about that itch, thinking perhaps it was unnatural. But he had long ago given up on worrying about that. Right or wrong, deranged or not, it was the way he was, and he had come to accept it.

As the days and weeks passed slowly by, Maxwell began to think more and more about leaving Saint Louis. In the meantime, he tended bar in the rancid Hog's Blood saloon, and broke up fights, while trying to stay out of them whenever he could. On his own time, he would spend time in the Hog's Blood or one of the other waterfront saloons. He partook of one or another of the many working women who plied their ages-old trade along the waterfront. He tried nearly every restaurant in Saint Louis, always looking for the familiar spicy food he was used to, but none ever was good enough.

He came to know a little of the many men who frequented the low waterfront dive, and in doing so learned which ones were more likely to cause trouble. There were a few he would have preferred never step foot in the Hog's Blood, but his boss wanted to keep allowing them in, since they were a good source of revenue, he said. Maxwell suspected it was more because Womack, the owner, was afraid.

However, Maxwell did have to admit that a good many of the most frequent troublemakers were relatively peaceful until they had had too much cheap, awful whiskey. By the time they started a fight, they had spent all they were going to spend for the night, and Womack no longer cared if Maxwell threw them out.

The worst of the lot was Clyde Throgmorton, a big, rough-and-tumble man who humbled or cowed just about everyone else along this section of waterfront. He was about six-foot-four and weighed just under two hundred twenty pounds. He had a mane of unkempt, long brown hair, a thick, far-drooping mustache, a stubbled face, and bloodshot brown eyes. He was fierce enough at any time, but when he had a bellyful of rotgut he was a wild man. He would take on any and all comers, and usually won. He had no reserve in him when he was in his cups, and fought like a maniac.

Maxwell had tangled with him a couple of times, though not in any serious way. Though only about five-foot-nine and one-seventy, Maxwell was not afraid of the much larger Throgmorton. He just figured that it was easier to let Throgmorton knock out everyone else and then, when Throgmorton was somewhat sated by his victory, escort him out.

So it seemed only right, somehow, that Throgmorton would provide Maxwell a way out of this fetid saloon, and this hellhole of a city.

It was a hellacious night in the Hog's Blood—business was hopping. Maxwell and four other bartenders could barely keep pace with all the demand for whiskey and beer. The din was horrendous, with gunshots frequently piercing the rest of the cacophony. At least the gunshots were going into the air, Maxwell figured, and thus into the log roof. He hadn't seen anyone drop from a gunshot, or anything else.

Plenty of the men were gambling, mostly at various card games, of which euchre was predominant. And with the turn and quiet slap of the cards, unheard even at the tables at which the game was being played, came loud arguments, shouts of derision, and whoops of victory.

In one of the infrequent and very brief lulls, when the entire saloon seemed to quiet down as if by prearranged signal, Maxwell turned to one of the other bartenders—Tom Sprague—and said, "I expect zere will be a powerful lot of trouble before zis night is over."

"I figure you're right, Jacques," Sprague said with a sigh. He was tired already, worn down by all the work and the expectation of trouble. He did not look forward to it. He was still recovering from the last fight he had had to break up a couple nights earlier. His face was a mess of discolored bruises and there were still a few crude stitches in a cut over his left eye. He had been hit with a chair, which had angered him considerably. Though groggy, he had managed to get to his feet, grab a pistol from someone, and shoot the offender in the arm. That cleared out the combatants, and Sprague was able to head to a doctor.

"Cheer up, *mon ami*," Maxwell said with a small

laugh. "Maybe zere won' be such a big fight as ze last time you're in one, eh?"

"Like hell," Sprague said with a grimace. "But I figure you can take care of any trouble that arises. I can stand back here and offer you all the encouragement you need."

"Well, *merci, mon ami,*" Maxwell said in mock appreciation. "Zat makes me feel . . . "

As if planned, the bedlam erupted again, and the bartenders once more tried to keep up with it all.

An hour or so later, with the saloon still going full swing, Maxwell heard a shout that rose above all the others, an angry, booming voice that carried authority and boastfulness. It was a voice that was used to sparking fear and obedience.

"Looks like Clyde's at it a bit early tonight," Sprague commented.

"Zat might be good, eh? 'E will beat up some men and be done wit' it. Zen, when 'e is flush with his victory, 'e will leave, and zen we will had peace."

"I hope you're right, Jacques," Sprague said doubtfully. "But he ain't been here nowhere near long enough to have worked up a good drunk, which don't bode so well, as far as I'm concerned."

Maxwell had thought of that, and it bothered him, but he had tried to put on a good face about it for his fellow barkeeps. But as he dispensed shots and bottles of whiskey and mugs and buckets of beer, he kept a close watch on the ruckus that had exploded across the saloon.

Not surprisingly, the saloon quieted down considerably, and the rush at the bar faded to just about nothing as the brawl progressed. The saloon patrons were far more interested in watching the fight—and in betting on it—than they were in drinking right at the moment.

Maxwell watched, too, as Throgmorton tossed man after man away from him. He was in a fine, bellowing rage now, and woe to the man who went up against him when he was in such a state.

The melee didn't last long before Throgmorton was out of victims. Still in thrall to his fury, he grabbed one young man who had not been involved in the altercation and began pounding the snot out of the suddenly howling, quickly groggy man.

"Merde!" Maxwell muttered. "Zis is gone too far." He hopped up onto the makeshift bar, swung his behind around, then dropped off on the other side. With long, purposeful strides, he headed toward where Throgmorton was still beating the young man. He had taken on a whole new air, one of solid, whiplike determination. Even the men who had made fun of his clothes—puffy, off-white shirt tucked into a pair of colorful wool pants, that were in turn tucked into knee-high black leather boots; a bright red sash around his waist; and a black, wide-brimmed hat with the left side pinned up to the crown and held in place by the plume of some colorful bird—could not bring themselves to do so now.

Maxwell stopped not far from Throgmorton. Standing with arms akimbo, he shouted, "Let zat boy be, *mon ami*." Getting no response, he repeated it, even louder, hoping the loud voice would somehow get through the man's rage. It didn't.

"Merde," Maxwell muttered again. He moved in

and slugged Throgmorton on the side of the jaw, instantly regretting it. The man's jaw was as hard as rock.

But it served its purpose. Throgmorton stopped pounding on the man and let him drop to the floor. "What in all goddamn hell did you do that fer?" he asked Maxwell, looking surprised.

"To got your attention, *monsieur*," Maxwell said flatly.

"Well, I reckon you got it, boy," Throgmorton said harshly. "Now, what did you want of me?"

"To stop pounding on zat boy zere before you killed him."

"He had it coming," Throgmorton grumbled.

"*Mais non*," Maxwell responded easily. He still hoped he could end this peacefully. He just wanted to get Throgmorton out of the saloon before he started any more trouble. He thought he might be able to accomplish that. "Zat boy 'ad not'ing to done wit' ze ruckus. 'E was just standing zere minding 'is own business."

"Are you callin' me a liar, boy?" Throgmorton demanded.

"*Mais non*," Maxwell said with a shrug. "I just t'ink you was confused and t'ought dis boy was involved."

Throgmorton thought that over for a few moments, looking for all the world as if that was a most difficult process. Then he shook his head, annoyed. "Still sounds like you're callin' me a liar, boy." He paused. "And I don't take kindly to such a thing."

Maxwell shrugged. "It's no matter to me what

you t'ought, *imbécile*," he said. "You 'ave been a t'orn in dis *homme*'s side since I got 'ere."

"I don't take much to bein' called names either," Throgmorton said. He seemed almost confused.

"Zen gone away from zis saloon now, *monsieur*. *Vite!* Quickly! And don' come back. Zat will settle ze problem."

"Why you Frog-talkin' little bastard," Throgmorton snapped. He sprang at Maxwell.

The bartender was not there, though. He had ducked, hopped to the side a little, then swept Throgmorton's feet out from under him with one of his legs. Maxwell stood, looking down at the sprawled Throgmorton. "I told you again 'ere and now to get out of ze 'Og's Blood."

"The hell you say, boy," Throgmorton growled as he rose to his full height and looked down on the considerably smaller Maxwell. "At least not till I've stove your head in, damn you."

"Well zen, you *gros boeuf*—big ox—let's got it over with, *ça va?* Zere is no use in waiting."

"That's just dandy with me, you dumb bastard." He spit in his palms and rubbed them together. "I'm gonna enjoy makin' mincemeat out of you." He lunged at Maxwell again. But when the Cajun tried the same maneuver as before, Throgmorton stopped, shifted his weight and kicked out. His boot caught a surprised Maxwell in the side.

"*Zut!*" Maxwell spat out. "Damn!" He rolled with it as best he could, taking himself out of range of the boot that Throgmorton tried to stomp him with. He got to his feet, probing his side gingerly. He decided that none of the ribs was broken, but it would be painful as all hell for a while. He'd had worse before, and would live with this.

Seeing that Throgmorton was about to launch another attack, Maxwell decided he needed to take the initiative. He charged forward and slammed his shoulder into Throgmorton's chest. The big man, not expecting it, was rocked back a few steps. Before he could catch his balance, Maxwell was on him, slamming powerful punches into Throgmorton's midsection and ribs. Each blow elicited a small grunt from his opponent.

Maxwell didn't think he was doing too much real damage to Throgmorton, but he hoped to at least wear this madman down a little. Instinctively, he sensed that Throgmorton was regaining his senses, and he moved to dart backward. But he was a second too late. Throgmorton's big right fist gave him a powerful impetus, sending him reeling backward until he crashed into the ring of men watching the fight. They kept him from falling, but he was still muddle-headed and wobbly when they impelled him forward, back toward Throgmorton.

Somehow Maxwell managed to stay out of the way of another thundering fist thrown by Throgmorton, as he lurched to the side a few steps and stopped, trying to get his bearings. He turned just in time to receive another big punch, though he was at arm's length, so it didn't have the impact it might have had. Still, coming on the heels of the first one, it left Maxwell unsteady, and his limbs not functioning very well.

Throgmorton hit him a few more times, sending him stumbling around in a circle, until he finally collapsed. He lay in a heap, trying desperately to breathe and to clear his head. He was not too frightened, not being lucid enough for that, but he knew he was in serious trouble.

"*Zut!*" he muttered as he pushed himself slowly to his feet. He stood there, weaving. But he managed a small grin, even though it hurt like hell. "Is zat ze best you can done, *monsieur?*" he asked sarcastically.

"I was just lettin' you have a bit of a rest to let you get your senses back so's you'll feel it more when I go poundin' on you again."

"Well, you can end your waiting anytime."

"If that's your pleasure." Throgmorton's expression had not changed throughout, and it was hard to tell if he was still angry or if he was enjoying himself. He closed in on Maxwell.

The bartender swiftly bent, tore the dagger from the sheath in his right boot top, and plunged it deep into Throgmorton's innards just as the big man latched on to him.

"You are not so big and strong now, are you, *monsieur?*" Maxwell said harshly as he twisted the dagger back and forth a little. He finally pulled the knife free and then sank it into Throgmorton's midsection again.

The big man slumped against him, almost toppling him with his weight. But Maxwell managed to shove him off and let him fall, while he yanked his dagger free from the bloody body. Throgmorton wasn't quite dead when he hit the floor, but he wasn't far from it.

Breathing heavily, aching throughout his body, Maxwell looked down at the soon-to-be corpse, and then at the crowd of men. "Tom," he said quietly, "got some of zese *monsieurs* to clean zis mess up. I am going back to my room now, *n'est-ce pas?*"

He really didn't care if it wasn't all right to Sprague or even Womack, the owner. He was through for the night, and that's all there was to it.

3

A week later, Maxwell's face was still as colorful as the wildflower-covered prairie, when he was approached by a medium-sized man with an overly large head and the ugliest countenance Maxwell had ever set eyes on.

Maxwell was sitting at a table in the Hog's Blood, sipping at a whiskey, still smarting from the hellacious drubbing he had taken a week ago.

Without ceremony, the newcomer grabbed a wooden chair, spun it around, and sat, arms on the chair back. "How're you doin', my friend?" he asked.

"Since when was somebody I don' ever seen before become *mon ami*, eh?" Maxwell countered.

"Jist tryin' to be friendly."

"*Bien*. I am all right."

"You look a fright," the man said.

"I am surprised by zat? *Mais non*." Maxwell was getting a little irritated. "Now, *monsieur*, who are you? And what did you wanted wit' me?"

"Name's Giles Elgood." The man held out his

hand. When Maxwell shook it without comment, Elgood resettled himself more comfortably in the hard wooden chair.

"*Et je suis* Jacques Maxwell," the bruised bartender said with a shrug.

"I know who you are. That's why I'm here."

"Well, zen, why don' you tell me what you wanted of me, eh? Zat might 'elp," Maxwell said just a bit sarcastically.

Elgood nodded. "I'm in the employ of Mister Manuel Lisa, and . . . "

"Who is zis *Monsieur* Lisa?" Maxwell asked disinterestedly.

Elgood looked surprised. "Why, he's the biggest trader in all of Saint Louis," he said. "He sure is. Maybe in all the West. He's the principal of the Missouri Fur Company."

"*C'est bon,*" Maxwell said cynically.

Elgood glared at Maxwell's dark face for a moment, not quite sure if the Cajun had insulted his employer. Then he let it go. It was not important.

"So what did zis grand *Monsieur* Lisa want of me?" Maxwell asked.

"I saw that fight you were in last week. Hell of a ruckus."

"*Mais oui.* I 'ave to agree wit' zat," Maxwell said, loosening up a bit. "But what does zat 'ave to do wit' zis *Monsieur* Lisa of yours?"

"Well, now, give me a chance to finish, why don't you," Elgood said rhetorically, trying to sound as if he was chiding Maxwell. "You handled yourself mighty well against such a big feller, and even though you got the tar whaled out of you, you didn't have no give-up in you. It was plain to see right off that you got plenty of sand in you, boy."

Maxwell shrugged.

"I told Mister Lisa about you, boy. And, well, he'd be interested in havin' you in his employ."

"For what?" Maxwell was a little intrigued.

"He's puttin' together another trappin' and tradin' brigade to go up the Missoura."

"What kind of trapping?"

"Beaver, boy. Beaver. They have plumb fine hides on 'em. The Europeans make top hats out of 'em."

"I don't knew nothing about zem beavairs, nor about trapping or trading."

"Don't matter none. Most of the men we hire don't know nothin' about such things either, though we usually have a few old hands, you might say. Boys who've been out there before and know what they're doin'."

"I don't know if zat sounded good to me or not," Maxwell said, mulling the idea.

"Hell, boy, there ain't nothin' to it. Me and some of the others'll teach you all you need to know." He paused, then added, "What we mostly need is men with some sand in 'em. Men who know how to handle themselves in a ruckus, men who know how to use their wits and their weapons to survive, whether you're facin' a fractious skunk in a sinkhole like this or a painted red Injin out in some mountain valley. You look like you've been through some tough times, and you've come through 'em all mostly unscathed. You'll do."

"I nevair fought ze red Innians, though," Maxwell said.

They can be powerful mean, boy, and don't you doubt it. Hard as a musket barrel and more fierce than any bear you ever seen. The most fearsome ones paint their faces all up in the wildest colors and such, and they can ride better'n anyone I ever saw. Even the little ones."

He paused a moment. "But don't you worry too much about that, Jacques," he added. "There's a many of the red sticks who are right friendly to white men." He smiled a little crookedly at Maxwell. "As far as those Injins're concerned, Jacques, you're a white man."

"Zey ever seen a man wit' black skin?" Maxwell asked, curious.

"Some of 'em, sure. First white men up the Missoura—a couple fellers named Meriwether Lewis and William Clark took a bunch of men up the river all the way to its source, and then beyond— had a black-skinned feller with 'em. And I'll tell you somethin', hoss, from what I heared, them squaws took a powerful likin' to that black feller."

Maxwell didn't know much about Indian squaws, though he had heard some talk about them. Either the men doing the talking were completely taken with Indian women, or they thought they were all whores, and cheap, dirty ones at that. Still, the idea of possessing one, even if just briefly, was quite interesting to Maxwell. He smiled a little. He had been looking for something adventurous to do, and this seemed as if it would do just fine.

Maxwell nodded. "Well, *mon ami*, if your *Monsieur* Lisa wants to 'ire zis *homme*, zen I will 'ave to say *oui*."

It was Elgood's turn to nod. "Welcome aboard, Jacques." The two shook hands, then Elgood pushed himself up. "I'll be in touch with you soon. We leave in less than a month."

"I'll be ready. You can found me 'ere, *monsieur*. Either working or just sitting 'ere like now."

Elgood nodded, then strolled out.

Maxwell watched the man leave, wondering just what he had gotten himself into. He was not afraid in any way, but he wondered if perhaps he hadn't made a mistake. Though Elgood had indicated that Maxwell would be a trapper and trader, it was all too possible that he would be forced into some form of wretched work, such as poling or cordelling the boats up the river, or some other kind of miserable task that was well beneath his skill and ambition. He vowed then and there that he would kill the first man who tried to force him into such contemptible labor. And he would take out any others who came after that man, whether it took a minute or a month.

Comfortable with his decision, Maxwell settled back into his hard chair and sipped his rum. The liquor was a lot better than it had been the first time he had walked into the Hog's Blood saloon. He had made sure that Womack brought in some better rum. Oh, the customers still got the rancid stuff Maxwell had first been served, but he was not about to drink such foul spirits.

Maxwell was beginning to wonder if perhaps Elgood had been lying to him. More than two weeks had passed since Elgood had lifted him, and yet he had seen no sign of the trapper.

But finally Elgood showed up. He elbowed his way through the smoke and din in the extremely busy saloon and stopped at the bar. When he got Maxwell's attention, he leaned over the bar and shouted in the bartender's ear, "We meet at first light tomorrow, just above where the Missoura confluences with the Mississippi. Almost in Saint Charles."

Maxwell nodded. "I'll be zere, *mon ami*. Now, I got work to be did." He went back to tending the clamoring crowd near the bar.

Elgood turned and pushed his way back through the crowd.

After finishing his turn at the bar that night, Maxwell went to his room and gathered his belongings. There wasn't much, but among them were some special keepsakes, and a few things he considered important. He packed them in a sack, and began walking north along the Mississippi. Several hours later, he managed to find someone to ferry him across the Missouri. He walked some more, this time slightly northwest along the Big Muddy. He found a place he thought would be the loading site. Moving into some willows nearby, he sat, rested his head on his pack, and fell asleep.

In much too short a time, he heard activity. He opened his eyes and glanced out beyond the trees. There were two keelboats and several pirogues—long, dugout canoes—and men had begun to gather. Maxwell wiped the sleep from his eyes, finding it didn't help much, swung his pack up onto his shoulders, and headed toward the other men. He was mighty thankful that a fire was going, coffee was on, and several men were cooking up some victuals for breakfast. Without asking, he grabbed a plate, loaded it with food, filled a tin mug with coffee. He squatted a little way off and dug in, grateful for the filling food and the hot, refreshing coffee.

Before long, a short, swarthy man, dressed in the best finery Saint Louis had to offer, climbed on a large wooden crate and stood there, resting lightly on an unnecessary cane. Elgood climbed up beside him, looking large and slovenly next to the company owner.

Elgood instructed the men where to go to be outfitted, and then began calling off names. When he got to Maxwell's, the quadroon stood and followed the shuffling line of men walking past other workers who were doling out equipment and supplies.

Maxwell rejected the pair of boots they tried to give him. He pointed to his own. "Zese are good. Zey ain't 'ad 'oles or not'ing."

The worker shrugged, unconcerned.

Maxwell did take the heavy wool pants that were proffered, and the long, blousy shirt, much like the one he was wearing. He also accepted the four-point Whitney blanket, tin mug, wooden canteen, and long, heavy skinning knife. He looked at the knife and saw the imprint of the manufacturer, and he nodded. "Ze British, zey ain't such good folks," he allowed to no one in particular, "but zey know 'ow to make a 'ell of a knife."

His next stop was for arms. He set his other

equipment on one end of the table, and took the flintlock pistol the employee handed him. He checked it over carefully. He was familiar with pistols—rifles, too—but he had more experience with pistols. The flintlock was not the best one ever made, but the lock was strong, sturdy, and had a powerful spring. He nodded and stuck the weapon in his belt.

The worker handed him a musket, and Maxwell looked that over, too. Then he held it out. "I want a rifle instead, *mon ami*," he said quietly, but firmly.

"Mister Lisa says you get a musket, so you get a musket. You don't like it, you take it up with him. Till then, get movin'. There's others waitin' to get their gear."

"*Mais non, mon ami,*" Maxwell insisted, his voice deeper and stronger. "I will not took zis piece of shit."

They argued some more before Elgood came over, followed by Lisa. "What's the problem here, boys?" Elgood asked.

"I tell zis *imbécile* zat I won't took zis piece of *merde* musket. I want a rifle. A real rifle."

"Why?" Elgood asked. He knew why, he just wanted to see if Maxwell gave the same reason or if he was just trying to be troublesome.

"A musket, 'e don't shoot so good. Anyone knows zat. I won' place my life in jeopardy by having not'ing but a musket when we 'ave to fought ze red Innians. Or 'unt ze buffalo like I heard ze men talk about."

Elgood fought back a grin. "Sully, give the man a rifle. And anyone else who wants one, if we got enough of 'em."

"Yessir," the man named Sully said. He put the musket down and went into a canvas tent behind him. When he returned, he had an armful of rifles. He set them on the table and handed one to Maxwell, who checked it over and then nodded.

"Zis is much better," Maxwell said. He picked up his other things and moved to the next table. There he was handed a shooting bag, into which he put two thin bars of lead, several extra flints, a bullet mold, a small roll of patch material, ball puller, short starter, patch knife, and a screwdriver. He also received a full powder horn, a smaller horn full of priming powder, a tin flask with each kind of the gunpowder, and a small tin of sperm oil for the weapons.

At the next table, Maxwell got two twists of tobacco, and a fire-making kit, complete with burning glass. Then he was allowed to pick several small, personal items. The selection was meager, but he choose a penknife, a small clay pipe, a bandanna, a wood-handled toothbrush, a small, hand-held mirror, a straight razor, and a chunk of shaving soap.

His last stop was at a pile of old, worn bags with shoulder straps. He rummaged through them until he found one that was not too bad off. He dropped all his personal items into the buckskin sack and slung it over his shoulder. Then he went to where he had been when the roster was called off.

There, with another tin mug of coffee close at hand, he squatted and began sorting through his equipment. He unpacked his new personal bag and then repacked it to his liking. He did the same with his shooting bag. He loaded his rifle and

pistol, then took all his other gear and stuck it into
his leather sack with the few things he had
brought from Saint Louis. He rolled up his new
blanket and tied it with buckskin thongs to the
satchel. Then he sat on a rock, shooting bag and
possible sack across his shoulders, his rifle leaning
against his thigh. He finished off his coffee and
waited.

Before long, the last of the men had passed
through the supply line and were sitting or kneeling
around the camp, checking and storing their new
belongings.

Then Lisa mounted the large crate again and
made a speech about the grand adventure which
they were about to undertake. Maxwell shut him out
moments after he had started. He had had more
than his share of adventures. He didn't need some
squat little Mexican telling him about them.

An hour later, the men were on the keelboats
and in the pirogues. Voyageurs who would propel
the boats up the river pushed off from the muddy
bank. The Missouri's powerful current caught the
boat Maxwell was on—the *Minataree*—and started to
shove it back toward the Mississippi.

Then the boatmen heaved forward on a cordelle
line and the keelboat came to a halt. Moments later,
it began moving upriver, ever so slowly.

Maxwell lounged on the flat roof of the low
cabin and almost smiled. This was certainly not the
type of boat, or water travel, he was used to.

4

The trip upriver was, for the most part, excruciatingly dull, though for the men such as Maxwell, who had been hired as trappers and traders, the work wasn't backbreaking. Maxwell and the other trappers mostly did the hunting. A group of them would go ashore each morning as the boats were departing, and hunt as long as needed to get enough meat to feed the entire crew. Then they would cart the meat—deer most often in these parts—to a spot along the river where the boats could put ashore. If it was near dark by then, they would just make their nightly camp. If not, the hunters would climb aboard. Once back on the boats, the hunters would skin and butcher the meat, if they hadn't done so before, throwing the innards and the other unwanted parts overboard.

On occasion, the trappers would be called on to help the struggling boatmen tow or pole the craft upriver in particularly troublesome places. The trappers hated such work, and they grumbled and cursed the whole time they had to perform it. But they did not really balk at doing it, since if they didn't, they would lose a lot of ground, as it were, in a hurry.

However, such demanding duty served to remind the trappers in a most potent way that they had it easy. Not a one of them wanted to do such work on a regular basis. It was intensely laborious, muscle-straining, strength-draining, dangerous work, and the trappers wondered in awe at how the boatmen could do it day in and day out.

The trappers not among a hunting party for the day would stay on the craft, ready to defend the vessels and the boatmen if an attack came. The men were exceedingly bored with such duty for the first couple of weeks, since the tribes along the Missouri, so close to civilization, were not all that prone to attacking boats traveling upriver. Not that those Indians never attacked the boats, so the men had to be on alert all the time, just in case.

But as the boats began edging into Arikara territory, Elgood warned the men to be even more alert, both on land while hunting and while on deck.

"Why?" one of the new, inexperienced trappers asked. He was a young man named Henry Thornton.

"The Arikaras are known to be considerably warlike," Elgood said. "And it ain't unheared of for them to attack boats like ours."

"Reckon that scares the pants off the likes of you, eh, boy?" one of the old hands said with a snort. Judd Shawcross had been upriver with Lisa's company three times before, and he considered himself an expert on everything about the trip. He was a crotchety man in his late twenties, and was very full of himself. Worse, he could not abide green fellows like Thornton and many of the others on this trip.

"I wouldn't say that," Thornton responded testily.

"Jist you wait till one of them painted savages comes tearin' at you, screamin' his goddamn lungs out, ready to split your sorry hide from the top of your noggin to bottom of your crotch. You'll shit your britches, boy." He laughed hoarsely.

"We'll jist wait till that happens, then, and see jist how poorly I do," Thornton said stiffly. "I might surprise you."

"Sure you will, boy. Sure you will." Shawcross's tone was decidedly disdainful. "You'll either turn tail and run or you'll sit there unable to move, boy. Either way, you'll get your scrawny ass kilt dead."

"Left ze boy alone, *imbécile*," Maxwell said quietly.

Shawcross glared at the Cajun. Maxwell posed something of a problem for Shawcross. While Maxwell was inexperienced as far as this venture went, it was obvious to the trapper that Maxwell was no stranger to hardship and danger. Because of that—and other reasons—Shawcross did not like Maxwell. The former slave reciprocated in kind.

"What are you, boy"—this last word was not usually an insult out here, but Shawcross's tone made it one—"his mother? Or maybe his . . . servant?" This last was an even bigger affront.

"I am neither, *ce la gomme salaud*—you useless bastard," Maxwell said flatly.

"I don't know what them damn foreign words

mean, boy, but I sure as hell know I don't like your tone," Shawcross snapped.

"And zis *homme* don't like to be insulted because of ze color of my skin, *ça va? Monsieur* Lisa and *Monsieur* Elgood don' 'ave no concern about zat, why should you, eh?"

"Because it's my business, boy. I don't have to work next to any man I don't take a likin' to."

"Zen don't work nex' to me," Maxwell said with a shrug. "Zat won' bother me none, *ça va?* But don' make a problem about my color."

Shawcross made a rude noise with his lips, then said, "And supposin' I feel like doin' so?"

Maxwell took a few moments before answering. "Zen I will took my dagger to you. I am vairy good wit' it, too. I will cut your eyes out first, since zey are so offended by my color. Zen, if you continue to 'arbor zis ill will toward me, I will cut away other parts of you."

"That keelboat'll take wing like a hawk before the likes of you could take me in a fight, knives or not, boy. Why, I . . . "

"That's enough of such foolishment, Shawcross," Elgood said. He had been sitting quietly since he had issued his warning.

"Hey, Cap'n, that's not fair. I . . . "

"Shut your flappin' hole, Shawcross," Elgood snapped.

Shawcross growled and shoved off, crossing the roof of the cabin and hopping down onto the deck.

When Shawcross was gone, Thornton sidled over to where Maxwell still sat. "I appreciate what you did for me, mister," he said.

"It was not'ing, *monsieur*," Maxwell said with a shrug.

"Don't say that. I'm afraid of Shawcross, and didn't know if he might take after me."

"You didn't show no fear, *monsieur*."

"Maybe not, Mister Maxwell, but . . . Well, I think he's right. The first time some Injuns come at me, I jist might soil my breeches."

"You would not be ze first man to do such a t'ing under zose circumstances, *mon ami*." He grinned. "Who knows, eh? Maybe zat will 'elp you out some—ze Innians, zey won' be able to get near you to killed you, *ça va*? Ze stink will keep zose red men away."

Thornton sat in shocked silence for a few moments, then laughed. "Maybe it would at that, Mister Maxwell. Maybe it would."

"Don' call me *Monsieur* Maxwell, *mon ami*. I am Jacques."

Thornton nodded. "Well, I'm still mighty obliged to you for comin' to my defense, Jacques."

Maxwell nodded.

As the journey continued, the old-timers began telling more tales of the scary Indians and wild beasts that they would encounter where they were going.

Some of the younger men grew frightened, beginning to wonder how they would fare in the face of such hazards, but Maxwell was not among them. Though he had never fought Indians, he feared no man. And he had no reluctance about telling the experienced men that.

Most of the old hands—and the new men, too were a little wary of Maxwell since his small run-in with Shawcross. They were not quite sure how to act around him. Like Shawcross, they knew him to be inexperienced in the fur business, but he carried a certain air of deadliness about him. So none of them challenged Maxwell when he stated that he was afraid of no one.

Except Shawcross, but he was somewhat subdued about it, not wanting to draw Elgood's ire. Elgood was the captain of this venture, and as such, held absolute power. While Elgood seemed a fair and reasonable man, the men were not sure how harshly he would deal with any infractions of the rules he thought most important. It was not something Shawcross wanted to find out just for the sake of belittling one quarter-black man.

So everyone settled into something of an uneasy peace as the boats continued to creep up the powerful river. The men grew more tense and wary the farther they went. The stories of hostile Indians spooked most of the new men, until they were even reluctant to go ashore to hunt.

Maxwell had no such qualms. He would rather be on shore, hunting, having something to do, than to be on the boats, waiting for an attack that never seemed to come. He thought that a little strange, considering how much he enjoyed being on the water. But he accepted it.

He most often went out hunting with Henry Thornton and another young man, Lucius Beecher. Thornton had taken to Maxwell ever since Maxwell had come to his aid against Shawcross. And Beecher, who had been friendly with Thornton right from the start, saw no reason not to deal with Maxwell.

Somewhere in the Dakotas, where the Missouri made a grand sweeping southwesterly curve, the small hunting party got a large surprise. And an unpleasant one at that.

While the men were walking westward, roughly along the river's course though some yards removed from the cliffs, mud, and tangled brush along the banks, a small war party of Gros Ventres of the Plains suddenly appeared out of the thickets to their left.

Maxwell's two friends dropped the deer carcass they were carrying on a long pole between them and prepared to run, but Maxwell was having none of that. "You landlubbing sacks of bilge, just stood your ground," the Cajun growled.

The force of Maxwell's will stopped them from running, though they still looked uncertain and decidedly worried. Maxwell looked over at the Indians, who were charging on foot. They were yet a short distance away. Enough time to get set, Maxwell figured. "Now, boys, heard me well," he said urgently. "I don' know not'ing about zese Innians, *mes amis,* but I don' t'ink zey are 'ere to 'ave us a party, *n'est-ce pas?*"

Neither Beecher nor Thornton understood half of Maxwell's words, but they got his drift, and they nodded, still scared down to their toes.

"We must done zis like we 'unt, *ça va?*" Maxwell continued. "One will shoot while ze others stay ready, understand?" When both nodded, Maxwell added, "While ze first is reloading, ze second 'e shoots his rifle. Zen ze t'ird. By zen, ze firot will bo reloaded."

"By then, they'll be on us," Thornton muttered.

"*Mais oui*, if zey don' turn tail and ran first. If zey are 'ere, zen we will fight zem with teeth and knives, eh?"

"I don't like the sound of that, Jacques," Thornton said.

"It don' matter what you didn't like or not, *mon ami*. It is what is, *ça va?*" He turned and faced the Indians. "Now, got ready. I will took ze first shot. 'Enry, you took ze second."

Without waiting to see if the others were really ready, Maxwell dropped to one knee, brought his rifle up, and fired. Through the billow of powder smoke, he saw an Indian fall, and was elated. He wasn't a bad shot, but he was still amazed.

His joy quickly faded, however, when he saw that the warrior got up right away and renewed his charge. "*Zut!*" Maxwell muttered. "*Merde et merde encore!*"

Despite his anger at himself, Maxwell was already beginning to reload, watching with half an eye toward the still-charging Indians. As he poured priming powder into the pan and snapped the frizzen shut, Thornton fired. This time a warrior went down and stayed there.

"I got one!" Thornton crowed.

"*Fermez la bouche et chargez un fusil!*" Maxwell snapped.

"Huh?" Thornton said, more confused than ever.

"Shut your fly trap and reload, you damn fool," Beecher yelled. He hadn't understood a word

Maxwell had said, but he knew damn well what the black meant.

Thornton hurried to do so, and just about the time Beecher fired, the Gros Ventres were upon them. Maxwell and Thornton each fired again, without aiming, and without much effect.

Maxwell was more in his element with this close-in fighting. He swung his rifle like a club, swatting down the first warrior to get within reach. The next Gros Ventre, however, was too fast and too sly, and managed to duck the swinging club. He surged in, and used a stone-headed club held in both hands and the shield strapped to his left arm to shove the rifle away and knock it out of Maxwell's hands.

As the warrior plowed into him, Maxwell tried to cushion the shock of landing. It still hurt when his back slammed onto the hard, spiky-grass ground, but he was able to slip the dagger out of his tall boot. The fight between Maxwell and the Gros Ventre was short but bloody. It ended with the warrior dead on the ground, covered with blood from two dozen dagger punctures.

Maxwell spun around, looking feral, hoping his friends were all right. They were just finishing off one of the warriors. They whooped in frightened victory as the three remaining Gros Ventres grabbed their dead and wounded companions and ran.

The three victors stood there, the two younger ones suddenly silent, realizing what had just occurred. Thornton turned to Maxwell and asked, tremulous amazement in his voice, "Did we jist take on an Indian war party and whup 'em?"

"Zat we done, *mon ami*," Maxwell responded with a tight grin. "I ain't certain, you understood, but I t'ink we kill two of zem red men. Maybe t'ree."

"Not bad for a couple of boys who're greener'n a new saplin'," Beecher said with just a touch of braggadocio.

"I agree," Maxwell said with a firm nod. "We t'ree, we make ze good team, eh?"

"That we do, Jacques," Thornton said. He was still stunned at all that had occurred here. He paused, then said, "But you know somethin', Jacques, I don't feel so good about all this. I mean, about killin' a man, even if he was a red-skinned son of Satan."

"It is nevair easy ze first time. It gots a little easier after zat, especially when ze man is trying to kill you. *Mais oui*. But you must beware," Maxwell warned his two young friends, "zat you don't come to like ze killing, and zat it gets too easy for you, *n'est-ce pas?*"

"I understand," Thornton answered quietly, as he and Beecher both nodded solemnly.

"Well, *mes amis*," Maxwell said, "we better grab ze deer meat and be on our way again. We still 'ave to meet ze boats up ze rivair somewhere."

"How the hell can you think of meat at a time like this?" Thornton asked, still looking a little queasy.

Maxwell shrugged. It had been a battle, and a small one at that. He could afford it no more time or attention. It was difficult for him to remember what it was like when he had been younger and had been called on to kill a man for the first time. Had he thought about it, he might have recalled being almost as queasy as Thornton was right now. On the other hand, his life had been filled with so many twists and turns, so much violence and adventure, that perhaps it had not bothered him at all at the time. Regardless, there were things to be done now. The men on the boats had to be fed, which he explained to his two young charges.

"They ain't gonna miss one damn deer," Thornton said with a bit of a sniveling.

"*Bien sûr que non*, Maxwell said with another shrug. "Of course not. But I don' t'ink you want to go back to ze boat and told *Monsieur* Elgood zat a few Innians scared you off from bringing home ze meat, eh? No, I don' t'ink you do."

"You're right about that, Jacques," Thornton said with a touch of contrition.

"I don't want to neither," Beecher chimed in.

He seemed a lot less ill at ease with this little episode, and Maxwell wondered about it a bit. Perhaps Beecher had killed before. Or maybe he was simply putting on a devil-may-care front to cover his uneasiness. But then Maxwell realized it didn't matter. It was not his place to concern himself about it. These two younger men would have to face these situations and deal with them as best as they could. If they didn't, they would die soon. Even though Maxwell had never been out here before, he knew that. It was the same whether on these sere plains or on a ship in the Gulf of Mexico. He would help them where he could, but he could not hold their hands and nursemaid them.

"And I think we ought to be gettin' a move on, boys," Beecher added.

"Why?" Thornton asked, turning toward his friend.

"I don't know any more about those Injuns than Jacques here does, and that means next to nothin'. But I figure that, was I them Injuns and I was close to home and jist got my ass whupped by some strange ol' boys, then I jist might go home and git some help and pay those strange ol' boys another visit."

"Your t'inking is *très bon*," Maxwell said. "So reload your weapons, *vite*, zen we will grab ze deer and got moving, eh?"

"Whatever you say, chief," Beecher said with a touch of friendly sarcasm.

"Zat's right," Maxwell said with a wide grin, "I am ze chief. Ze big chief, and don' you boys forgot zat." He laughed, and the others joined in.

As they marched on, Maxwell more careful, each assessed his wounds. All had some small cuts and scrapes, but that seemed to be about it. Maxwell could feel a small knot growing on his back where he had hit a rock when he had been dumped by the Indian, but he hardly noticed it once he had made note that it was there.

Several hours later, Maxwell, who was in the lead, and more alert than he ever had been, spotted two buffalo not far off. He continued to trudge along, thinking. He finally decided to take a large chance. He didn't know why, he just accepted the fact that his mind had made the decision for him, and he would stick with it.

"*Mes amis,*" he called softly. When the two friends trudged up, he said, "I am going to shoot one of zem buffalo. Maybe ze bot' of zem."

"You're deranged, Jacques," Beecher said. "We cain't carry all that meat."

"I know zat," Maxwell said with a snort. "What I plan for you to did is to take ze deer meat to a place for ze boat, zen bring back some of ze men to 'elp carry ze meat back."

"And what're you gonna do while we're busy with that?" Thornton asked.

"I will be butchering ze buffalo, *ça va?* I will keep my rifle 'andy, and if more Innians show up, I can use ze buffalo carcass to hide behind, eh?" He made it sound so simple.

"Now I know you're deranged," Beecher said, but there was a note of admiration in his voice.

"Maybe, *mon ami.* But I 'ave decided to done zis, so shoo. Bring me some 'elp as soon as you can."

Shaking their heads, the two young men headed off as quickly as they could, the deer carcass swinging merrily on the pole between them.

Maxwell watched them for only a moment. Then he walked forward, head held high. He had hunted buffalo before, in larger groups. But he had never done so alone. And with the group, most of the men thought they must creep up on the great shaggy beasts. He wanted to see if that was necessary. While he thought the bison a magnificent animal, he suspected that it was in most ways not too smart.

He got to within fifty yards of the two beasts before they started getting edgy, snuffling warily. Maxwell stopped, checked his priming, and fired. One buffalo started as a puff of dust rose from its fur, and it staggered a bit. Then it shuffled off, its ungainly gait made worse by the lead ball lodged deep in its vitals. The second one followed.

"*Merde, merde, merde,*" Maxwell spat. He blew down the barrel of the rifle to make sure no embers still burned there. Then he took off running after the buffalo, reloading on the run.

He stopped when he was almost a hundred yards away from the two animals, who had come to a halt.

The buffalo he had shot was wavering considerably, and looked ready to fall, but he could not take the chance that it was done for. He fired again, and the beast went down, kicking feebly for a while.

Maxwell stood where he was, reloading again while keeping his eyes open for hostile Indians. He realized it had probably not been the wisest thing for him to do, to fire two shots when he had fought off an Indian attack only a few hours earlier. He shook his head in annoyance at himself, but he grinned with a bit of rue. "And to t'ink, *Monsieur* Jacques Maxwell, ze great huntair, zat you was t'inking zat ze buffalo was ze stupid one 'ere. *Zut!*"

He finally approached the animal and jabbed it a few times with the muzzle of his rifle, just to make sure. Certain that the bison was dead, Maxwell looked around. The other buffalo was placidly eating grass, as if nothing had happened. There was no sign of Indians that he could see. Maxwell leaned his rifle against the warm, furry carcass, where it was readily available, then drew his butcher knife and set to work.

While he hacked and cut at the thick hide, and meat, he kept scanning the horizon for any signs of Indians. Or of help. The latter finally arrived almost three hours after he had shot the buffalo. He ducked behind the mostly butchered carcass when he first heard the approaching group. When he was sure it was his friends, he stood and began wiping his bloody, greasy hands on tufts of harsh grass and handfuls of dirt.

"It's about time you all got 'ere," Maxwell said sarcastically as the others trod up.

"Go to hell, you dumb bastard," Judd Shawcross said nastily. "This was one goddamn stupid thing you done here, boy. Was it left up to me, I'd never have sent this party out here to get your scrawny ass and to drag that disease-ridden ol' buffler carcass back to the boats."

"But it was not left up to you, eh?" Maxwell said evenly. "Ze decision was left to one wit' brains in his 'ead. So, stop your complaints and have ze men get ze meat back to ze boat, *monsieur*."

Shawcross scowled at Maxwell for a few moments, but then turned and began issuing orders to his men.

It was past dark when they reached the camp and the boats. Elgood was worried that perhaps he had lost more than half his men on this ill-advised venture. He sighed with relief when they marched wearily into camp.

Most of the men were happy to have the buffalo meat. They were plumb sick of deer meat and fish by now, and some fire-seared hump meat or ribs would go down mighty nicely.

Elgood could see that the men were worn down by all the work they had been through on the trip, and he magnanimously agreed that this night would be for a feast, and that the men could take it a little easier the next day. That brought a cheer.

It also brought an anonymous comment out of the darkness: "How's about you break out a jug or two for the festivities, Cap'n."

Elgood thought it over for perhaps two blinks of an eye. "Sounds like a plumb fine idea to me, boys. Get that buffler meat a-cookin' and I'll fetch up a couple jugs for us."

As the night progressed, and the buffalo meat and liquor went down, Maxwell let his two companions of late tell the story of their fight with the Indians.

"What kind was they?" one young man asked, interested, just after the tale began to unfold.

"Hell if I know," Beecher said with a shrug. "Jist painted savages that was out to kill us."

"They was out for hair and plunder, includin' that deer meat you boys had," Elgood opined. "What did they look like, Jacques?" he asked, figuring that Maxwell would have been the most observant of the three.

"I can't say too well, *Monsieur le Capitaine*. I was a bit occupied, *n'est-ce pas?*" He grinned. "But I could seen zey were vairy unfriendly, *ca va?*"

"Understood," Elgood said with a laugh. "I expect they were Gros Ventres of the Plains," he added. "They often loiter in these parts and cause trouble for unwary travelers like you boys."

"Whatever they was," Thornton said truthfully, "I don't never want to face 'em again. They were mean varmints."

"Chicken-hearted bastard, jist like I thought from the start," Shawcross said in uncharitable tones. "All three of you are the same. Scared out of your wits at everything."

"Damn you," Beecher snapped. "You know better than that."

"Do I?" Shawcross responded with a sneer. "What kind of proof do you have, boy? I don't see no scalps hangin' from your belts. I don't see no wounds, 'ceptin' fer a couple of scratches you likely got whilst you were scramblin' through the thickets tryin' to scare up a deer."

"That ain't so," Thornton protested loudly. "It went jist like me and Lucius said it did. Ain't that right, Jacques?"

"Ain't no one here gonna believe that black-skinned varmint no more'n any of us ol' hands believe you two young, green snots," Shawcross said, even more harshly than before.

Thornton and Beecher continued to protest the notion that they had made up the story, but the angrier the two got, the more incoherent they became. Until finally they were red-faced and tongue-tied, unable to get out an understandable sentence. Both looked at Maxwell, pleading with their eyes for him to do something to help them out of this morass of their own making.

Maxwell had listened to it for a while, letting Shawcross play his game, since the trapper had mostly left him out of it except for a crack or two here and there. Finally, though, seeing how flustered the two young men were, he decided that his new friends had had enough. They were good men, he figured, just young and inexperienced, and Maxwell could see that Shawcross had a plain nasty streak that he was using to take advantage of Thornton and Beecher.

"You don' believe what zese *monsieurs* said, *Monsieur* Shawcross?" Maxwell asked in quiet, flat tones that brought the merrymaking to a halt.

"Hell no, I don't believe those lyin' bastards," Shawcross snapped, eyes glaring in the firelight.

"Zen you are calling me a liar, too, you fish-'umping land 'og?" Maxwell asked calmly.

"And if I am?" Shawcross responded with another sneer. He rose, figuring the time had come to eradicate this pest.

Maxwell smiled tightly, and also rose. Then, before Shawcross could say another word, Maxwell kicked his feet out from under him and was kneeling on his chest, the sharply pointed tip of his dagger brushing Shawcross's throbbing carotid. "Ze nex' time you said somet'ing like zat to me," he said evenly, though with no doubt as to his seriousness, "I'll kill you till you were dead, *monsieur*."

"That ain't fair," Shawcross protested, gasping from Maxwell's weight on him. "You took me by surprise."

"Jus' like zem Indians did to us."

"You gimme a fightin' chance, you barbarous son of a bitch, and I'll stomp your black ass into the ground."

"Zen by all ze means, why don' you try to did zat," Maxwell said, rising and sliding the dagger away. "But you best understood zis, *monsieur*—zis ol' frain of Jean Lafitte ain't gonna did no fighting for fun. *Mais non!*"

"Friend of who?"

"Jean Lafitte, ze great pirate."

"Never heard of him, boy," Shawcross said, getting up while keeping a wary eye on Maxwell. He brushed dirt off him. "But it don't matter none nohow. I don't give a pig's snout if you're a friend of President Madison hisself, I'm still gonna carve you into pieces so small nobody ain't ary gonna find 'em all again."

Maxwell shrugged. "Zen come and did it," he

said calmly. By his tone, he could've been ordering a beer back at the Hog's Blood in Saint Louis.

"Hold on there, boys," Elgood barked, taking command of the situation. "I don't want none of my men killin' another. We need every hand we got."

"Piss on that, Cap'n," Shawcross snapped. "This fractious bastard's got to be taken care of before he causes trouble for the whole crew."

"It's you who'll cause all ze trouble," Maxwell said, still calmly. But he, too, wanted it over with. He was certain he could take Shawcross, and he wanted to get it out of the way so he would not have to worry about looking over his shoulder all the time.

"You two bound and determined to go at each other?" Elgood asked.

Each man nodded.

"Damn," Elgood breathed in annoyance. He didn't want to sanction this foolishness, but he knew that if he didn't, it would only get worse. "All right then, fellers, you can do so, but it's gonna wait till mornin'. If you're determined to try'n kill each other, I want it as fair as can be. That means I want you both sober and facing the light of day. Maybe after a full night's sleep you'll think differently."

"Ain't likely," Shawcross growled.

Maxwell just shrugged, and headed for his blanket.

6

A somber group of men gathered the next morning around an area they had just cleared. At one side of the makeshift arena stood Maxwell; across from him stood Shawcross. The former seemed at ease, relaxed, confident; the latter was tense, angry, and seemed to be growling to himself.

Elgood stepped into the center of the open space and looked from one combatant to another. "You boys still aim to follow through on this idiocy?" he asked.

Maxwell shrugged. He didn't care much either way.

Shawcross, however, was firm. "Damn right I want to go through with it. It's long past time that mouthy bastard got what was comin' to him."

"You realize, don't you, Judd, that it might be you who gets his comeuppance?" Elgood noted.

"Ain't goddamn likely, Cap'n."

Elgood shook his head at the man's arrogance and obstinacy. Shawcross was going to get himself killed for no good reason. Elgood sighed. Well, the decision was out of his hands now. Actually, as the captain of this expedition, he could order them not to go through with this. But that, he knew, would do nothing but delay the inevitable. At least this way it would be as fair as he could make it. He hated to lose either man, but Shawcross had, over the past couple of years, become so troublesome that Elgood almost hoped it was the crusty trapper who came out the worse for this fight. Not that Elgood figured Shawcross stood much of a chance. There was something about Maxwell that made Elgood think the black was a lot more formidable than he seemed.

"Anythin' either of you wants to say before this fracas commences?" Elgood asked.

Each combatant shook his head. Maxwell pulled his old cloth shirt off and dropped it to the ground. A nasty, massive scar disfigured one shoulder.

Shawcross spat, then followed suit, not wanting to be outshone in showing off his musculature. He didn't realize that his pasty whiteness looked sickly and pale in contrast to Maxwell's light caramel coloring.

"Then," Elgood said with reluctance, "you best commence." He stepped back, until he was just one of the men in the crowd.

As Maxwell and Shawcross moved warily toward each other, a man named Pete Lepari shouted, "I got two dollars cash money says the Negro feller wins. Any takers?"

There were plenty, and within a heartbeat, men were wagering whatever small bits of cash they had, knives, small personal items, anything they could come up with that had any value at all. They had often played cards on the journey, but this—this was real wagering, and something new besides.

The sudden swell of noise startled both opponents, who stopped and looked around in surprise at the wagering men. Then they shrugged, and went back to approaching each other, minds back on the work at hand. Both ignored the shouting and yelling that continued once the bets were placed, as the men cheered for the combatant they had wagered on.

Maxwell had long ago sized up Judd Shawcross as a bully and a blowhard, someone who intimidated people through a fierce-looking exterior, not through his skill as a brawler. So Maxwell was not all that worried about Shawcross, but he remained wary. He knew that if he let down his guard for even a moment, Shawcross would be all over him.

Maxwell took the initiative and charged. He figured that he could get this over with in a hurry if he made Shawcross fight on his terms. Shawcross was surprised, having thought that Maxwell would wait for him to attack. But he recovered well, he thought, and blocked the looping left fist Maxwell launched at his head.

In doing so, however, Shawcross missed Maxwell's booted foot, which crushed his genitals.

He howled and bent in half, clutching at his mashed testicles. He sucked in great draughts of breath, trying to ease the agony.

"Dumb bastard," Maxwell said, shaking his head a little. He stepped up, then slammed his locked fists down on the back of Shawcross's neck.

The trapper crumpled. Maxwell moved in and began battering Shawcross, punching and kicking him.

Finally Maxwell stepped back, giving Shawcross a breather. "'Ave you 'ad enough, *monsieur?*" he asked haughtily. "Are you ready to been a reasonable man, or is zat too much for an *imbécile* like you, eh?"

Shawcross got groggily to his feet. He was woozy, and he felt as if his body was in flames from all the aches he had suffered at Maxwell's hands. But now that he was up and had had a few minutes' relief from the thumping, he was beginning to feel a little better. At least enough to be able to fight back some. If he could get a few more moments to recover, he figured he would be all right.

"What's zis?" Maxwell said mockingly. "Ze great Judd Shawcross has not'ing to said? Ze big blowhard who is always telling everybody what *un grand homme* 'e is can't found any words?"

Maxwell's scornful little speech gave Shawcross the few moments more of respite he wanted. He drew in a deep breath and let it out slowly. "Piss on you, Maxwell, you mongrel son of a bitch." Shawcross drew his knife and suddenly came at Maxwell.

Maxwell grabbed the wrist of Shawcross's knife hand in both his hands and twisted his foe's arm down, around and up along the back. There he found it easy to pluck the blade from Shawcross's fingers. "You are too stupid to continue living, *monsieur*," Maxwell said harshly into Shawcross's ear. "Much too stupid." Without remorse or hesitation, Maxwell ran the blade of Shawcross's own knife against Shawcross's throat, opening up the carotid arteries.

When Shawcross had finished gurgling, Maxwell dropped the body to the ground, then dropped the knife next to the corpse.

Men cheered or groaned as they collected or paid their bets. Those who had favored Shawcross were shocked, not so much that he had lost, nor even that he had lost to a black man, but that it was over in roughly a minute from start to finish, including the unmerciful beating Maxwell had given his opponent.

Elgood walked up to Maxwell. He, too, was a little surprised at the swiftness and brutality of Maxwell's attack. "Goddamn, boy," he said. "That was some exhibition you put on there, son."

Maxwell shrugged. He felt no regret at having killed Shawcross, but he was not a man who got any enjoyment out of another man's demise, especially when he had caused it.

Elgood had hoped Maxwell would open up a little and talk about himself, but apparently that was not going to happen. He hesitated, then made his decision. "We're short a man now," he said quietly, "and a brigade leader to boot." Then he grinned harshly at Maxwell. "But what the hell, boy, since it was you who went and killed that crusty bastard, you can just replace him as a brigade leader."

It was Maxwell's turn to be shocked. He wasn't sure he had heard right, and didn't know that he wanted to hear right. "I don' know 'ow to did any trapping," he said tentatively.

"Then you'll just have to learn, won't you, son?" Elgood responded, almost enjoying the discomfort on Maxwell's face. "And goddamn fast, too, I'm sayin' to you."

"You're an evil man, Cap'n," Maxwell said, meaning it at the moment. He was beginning to think that he might have to place a little curse on Elgood. Not that he didn't like Elgood. He did, but he thought this was a low thing for Elgood to do to him, and he felt it should be addressed. He remembered the slaves back on the plantation would have placed a curse on someone for such an offense. But he was not versed in those arts, nor was he sure he would want to use such power.

"Hell I am," Elgood said somewhat cheerfully. "I just think it's fittin' that you take over for Shawcross. I see it as justice inspired by God and his good grace."

"Did you evair t'ink maybe zis is a mistake? I'm not a man who likes much responsibility, *ça va?*"

"I could be makin' a mistake," Elgood admitted. "But I don't really reckon so. You've shown me you got sand in you, son. You're tougher than dried rawhide, and mighty resourceful, too. That's a good combination for a brigade leader. And, hell, most of the men like you, son." He grinned. "That ain't somethin' I'd have expected."

"Me either, *Capitaine*," Maxwell said in disgust at having been put in this position. He could, he knew, just plain refuse to take the proffered position, but he figured that was a good way to face censure. Elgood would not be happy if he was refused, and Maxwell didn't want to find out what the captain would do.

"Well, son, then it's set," Elgood said. He had an idea of what Maxwell was thinking, and he wanted to make sure Maxwell had accepted it. If so, it would head off trouble.

Maxwell's lips and splayed nose twitched a little as he fought back a retort. Then he said, "Reckon it is, *Capitaine*. Not zat it gives me any enjoyment, *ça va?*"

"Doesn't matter much whether you like it or not, just as long as you do it. And do it well."

"*Mais oui*, I'll do it, *Capitaine*. And I will do my best. 'Ow good zat will be, though, who can said," he added with a shrug of his shoulders.

Elgood was relieved. He turned to look at the men, who were still gathered around, watching and listening intently now. "You boys have any objections to Mister Maxwell here leadin' one of our trappin' parties, now that Judd's gone under?"

One or two men looked as if they might voice a complaint, but then they decided it would be far better to just keep their mouths shut.

"Then it's done. Any of you who were supposed to work with Shawcross and don't want to do the same with Mister Maxwell, see me and we'll make some arrangements. If there's anyone assigned to someone else's crew and wants to work with Jacques, let me know."

"I want to work with Jacques," Thornton said immediately.

"And me," Beecher tossed in.

Both young men were quite impressed with Maxwell, though at the same time they were more than a little frightened of him. Still, after seeing how well he had handled himself against the Gros Ventres, and now against Shawcross, they were certain he was someone to be followed. He had, as Elgood had pointed out, displayed considerable toughness and resourcefulness. And more importantly to the two young men, he had made them stay and fight the attacking Indians. If he had not, they would have had to live with the knowledge that they had run as soon as real danger had reared. This way, they knew they could hold their own against the Indians, and therefore, pretty much anyone else. That made them somewhat proud of themselves, and they owed that to Maxwell.

"You mind takin' on these two boys, Jacques?" Elgood asked.

"I don' know about doing such a t'ing, *Monsieur le Capitaine*." Maxwell said. "I t'ink zey will do not'ing but cause trouble for me. Zey are just boys, *ça va*? And so zey will keep needing me to got zeir *derrieres* out of ze fire. I don' knew if I 'ave ze time for zat."

Thornton and Beecher were crestfallen, and looked at each other, trying not to cry or snivel at the disparaging words about them.

Then Maxwell grinned widely. "But I'll take zem on anyway. Someone 'ere will 'ave to make sure zey don' get in trouble. Since zey want to join me, I don' t'ink it's right for me to gave zem and zeir troubles to someone else, eh?"

"We won't cause you no troubles, Jacques," Thornton said eagerly. "Really. Right, Lucius?"

Beecher hesitated, then smiled a little. "He's jist

joshin' us, Henry," Beecher said. "He don't really think we'll cause him all that much trouble. No more'n anyone else, anyway."

"That right, Jacques?" Thornton asked hopefully.

"*Oui*. Zat is true. Actually, I am 'appy to 'ave you two *avec moi*. I 'ave seen you fight *les* Innians *sauvages*, and I know you are brave men. Zere is no one who can argue about zat wit' me." Though Maxwell realized he knew nothing of trapping or of the western lands where they were going, he was certain he could teach the two how to be tough and resourceful enough to face whatever those lands would throw at them in the coming months. So he didn't mind taking them under his wing, even if only to prove himself as a mentor of sorts. But that was not the only reason. He found them quite companionable, if perhaps a bit naive and talkative at times, but he could put up with that to have two men he was pretty sure he could rely on.

With that settled, Elgood turned and ordered several of the men to see that Shawcross was buried. When that was done, the leader said a few words over the simple, shallow grave—a rite that less than one-quarter of the men attended—and then auctioned off what few personal goods Shawcross had called his own. Most of Shawcross's possibles reverted to the company, but the rest went to the men who had won some cash money on the wagering, or had had a few coins stashed away.

The sale was over quickly, and the men gathered around, awaiting new orders. Elgood thought about it, then climbed up on a stump. "I told you boys last night during the festivities that we'd stay here today to let you recover from all the feastin' and such." He smiled a little. "And it looks like more than a few of you can use the respite."

Several groans from men who were suffering hangovers proved Elgood's statement. "I don't see any reason why I should change that just because of this mornin's occurrence. So you're free to do what you will, as long as you don't mosey off somewhere and don't cause no troubles. Enjoy yourselves, boys, for it ain't likely you'll get another chance to do so anytime soon."

Elgood stepped down and then hunted up Maxwell. He found the black sitting at a fire with Thornton, Beecher, and the four other men who would make up his small trapping party. "Mind if I set a spell?" Elgood asked.

"Mais non," Maxwell said, though without much enthusiasm. He was still more than a little angry at Elgood, but he figured he should be polite to his boss.

"I didn't want to say anything about it in front of the others before, Jacques, though I hinted at it. I figure now's the time for me to ask. As I said, I noticed in your fracas with Shawcross, and back in the Hog's Blood's in Saint Louis, that you seem to handle yourself mighty well in close quarters."

"Oui, I do," Maxwell said without braggadocio. "And what of it, *monsieur?"*

"I'm mighty curious as to how you got to be that good. You ain't a slave. Or, if you were, it's been a time. And there ain't too many places where a black man can learn to handle himself in a fight like I've seen you do. So how did you learn it?"

"I t'ought men like me, like any of dese men here, weren't asked such questions, *Capitaine*," Maxwell said quietly.

"That's true in most cases, son," Shawcross responded soothingly. "But you ain't exactly a usual case, now are you?"

"*Mais non*." Maxwell smiled a little while he thought. Then he said, "So I will told you. I was a slave, yes, ze son of a plantation owner in Louisianne and a 'alf-Creole, 'alf Cajun slave. Ze mastair, 'e would not recognize me as his son, *bien sûr*—of course—and my life as a youngster was vairy bad."

Spring 1810

Young Jacques Maxwell's childhood was one of beatings, whippings, backbreaking labor, and the worst degradations imaginable. His lot was no worse than any other slave's, and certainly no better. But since it was all he knew, he thought he was destined to live this way until he died.

However, on his infrequent trips to pick up supplies in town, he could see something of how white people—other than plantation owners—lived. Even the worst off of them had it infinitely better than he did. Maxwell also became aware that the few freed blacks he saw had a life considerably brighter than his, though even those men and women still faced appalling humiliations every day. Still, to a young Jacques Maxwell, their lives looked a lot better than his own, and he envied those people. He wondered how they had gotten their freedom, and he sometimes dreamed of having it himself.

He could see no way of gaining his freedom other

than running away. But he had seen what happened to slaves who had fled and been recaptured. The punishment was far more than he was willing to pay for an uncertain future as a freed black man in a white man's world. He had heard whispered stories of people of his color living lives of relative freedom and even prosperity in states far to the north, but he decided those were tall tales, told by slaves to ease the burden of their wretched existence.

But when he was fourteen, his mind changed about trying to find a way to freedom.

His mother, a handsome woman the color of café au lait, was the master's favorite. She had already borne him six children, though she was not yet twenty-five. She had also surreptitiously fallen in love with another Haitian-Creole slave, Henri Batteau, and had become impregnated by him. The master, Ambrose Maxwell, who had been away from the plantation for some months, was enraged when he learned that Maxwell's mother, whom he called Eve, was with child from someone else.

Ambrose Maxwell had two of his overseers drag Eve out of her shanty. The obviously pregnant woman screamed and kicked wildly, trying to break free. Her struggles only sufficed to amuse the white men. The two overseers dropped Eve at Maxwell's feet.

"Who put this child in yo' belly, woman?" Ambrose demanded.

"I don' know dat, *maître*," Eve answered tearfully. She was terrified, knowing that there was virtually no way she would escape some horrible punishment. But in that realization came a determination, too. She vowed to herself and to her voodoo spirits that she would not reveal Batteau's name, no matter what they did to her.

"You've been layin' with every man in the slave quarters?" Ambrose asked disdainfully. "That why you don't know whose goddamn pickaninny you're carryin'?"

"*Mais non, maître,*" Eve said quickly. She had not planned on this.

"'Cause if you been doin' so, there's gonna be a mess of my slaves who ain't gonna be sirin' no more little black bastards."

Eve was horrified. She knew Ambrose would easily carry through on his threat to castrate every slave he thought might have fornicated with her. She desperately wanted to think of something to end that threat but still protect her real lover. She felt a rush of relief when an idea suddenly popped into her head. In a heartbeat she tried to think of any bad implications for her or those she cared for, but she could not come up with any. She had to try it.

"It was Toby, *maitre,*" Eve said, hoping she would be believed.

"Toby, my house nigger?" Ambrose asked, stunned.

"*Mais oui.*"

"But why in hell would he . . ." Ambrose could not figure it out. Toby held one of the softest jobs a slave could have, working in the large plantation house for the master and his family. His chores were few and light, he dressed in finery, he ate well on the leftovers of the master and his family and guests, he even had his own small room in the house.

From where she still lay, looking up at Ambrose,

Eve said, "'E was *jaloux* of you, *maître*. *Mais oui*. 'E saw that you 'ad me at any time, and 'e decided 'e wanted me 'imself. 'E did not t'ink you would learn of it, and if you did, 'e would deny it. He said zat you wouldn't believe my word against 'is. I believed 'im."

"What makes you think I'll believe you now?" Ambrose asked.

Eve was ready for that one. "Because I'm trying to save my life, *maître*. And ze life of my chil'."

Ambrose thought that over for a moment. Eve could be lying, he thought, but he didn't think that was likely. He was certain she did not have the capacity to concoct such a story. Still, he had trusted Toby for a long time, but he thought he could remember the look of desire and hate in Toby's eyes on occasion. He looked at a young slave boy. "Go fetch Toby for me, boy," he ordered.

The youngster ran off, eyes wide with fear. He returned in a few minutes with a tall, very dark-skinned man in his mid-thirties. Toby was, as usual, dressed in his house clothes: clean white jacket over a crisp white shirt and small black tie, good pants, and polished low-topped boots.

"Yessir, Massah Maxwell," Toby said. His voice held his normal tone of obsequiousness.

"I don't much care to be hoodwinked by any of my darkies, especially a house nigger I've put my trust in," Ambrose said coldly.

"What you mean, massah?" Toby asked, fright suddenly springing into his face. "I ain't evah deceived you, massah."

"Don't lie to me, you simple bastard," Ambrose

seethed. He turned to his two overseers. "Geld him," he said in tightly controlled anger.

The two white overseers grinned. It was almost as much fun for them to castrate a black man as it was to hang one.

Toby stood there, too shocked—and too ingrained in his life as a slave—to even protest, to ask why this was being done. He just simply could not believe this. He looked pleadingly at Ambrose, hoping to observe in the master's eyes that this was all a cruel hoax. But the icy glint of rage was all he could see.

One foreman kicked Toby's feet out from under him while the other shoved hard on the slave's shoulder. As soon as Toby landed in the dirt, the two whites knelt and sliced off Toby's trousers.

It was then that Toby regained enough sense to protest. "Don't let 'em do this to me, massah!" he screamed. "I ain't been disloyal to you, massah. Not in no way. Massah! Massah, stop 'em, please!"

He continued to scream as one overseer grabbed his genitals and the other made a swift sweep with a sharp knife. The two whites stood and the one showed off Toby's severed sex organs to the gathered slaves before he dropped the messy pile on Toby's chest.

Still lying on the ground at her master's feet, Eve felt sick. She had hated Toby with all her heart. Almost as much as she hated Ambrose Maxwell. That's why she had come up with the story that he was the father of the child growing inside her. She had hated his arrogance, and his life of relative ease. She had hated the fact that he took any of the women he wanted from the slave quarters—except for her, of course. He was too frightened of the master's favorite. She also hated the contempt he showed for the common slaves, acting as if he were one of the white bosses who ran the plantation under the overseers.

Despite all that, she was sick at what had just been done to Toby. She wanted to scream and tell them all it had been a mistake and to put Toby back together again. Then she remembered why she had done what she had. If she had said it was Batteau, then her lover would be the one lying there with his manhood gone. And perhaps Ambrose would have killed her and perhaps emasculated some of her four sons. Or worse, if she had refused to name anyone, the master would make good on his threat to start castrating the men until she did say something.

None of that took away the disgust and horror she felt. But she was still glad that it was Toby rather than Batteau lying there like that. And the horror would fade, she thought. She had seen such things happen before. The only thing that had made this worse than those other times was the fact that she was responsible for this instance. She hoped she could manage to overcome her mortification.

So occupied with those dreadful thoughts was she that Eve didn't really even feel the first kick to her bulging belly. It was only with the second hard kick a moment later that she realized what was happening to her.

She opened her eyes and looked up. Ambrose was leading his two overseers in kicking her. Boots slammed into her pregnant abdomen, and her back and her head. She cried hard, but tried to keep quiet. She did not want to scream because she thought that would only cause her tormentors to increase the ruthlessness of their onslaught. So she bore the attack as quietly as she could, praying to her voodoo gods to end the hideous assault she was undergoing.

Eventually it did come to a halt. Eve opened her eyes again and looked up. "Let that be a reminder to you, woman," Ambrose said in the most contemptuous voice he could muster. "Next time you take it into your nappy goddamn head to bed down with some stallion, you just remember what happened here today, because the next time, it'll be far worse for you and all the rest of your kind."

Eve nodded, not sure she was able to speak. Her body was aflame with pain, and she thought she could feel blood seeping from her private parts.

Then the whites were gone. Eve tried to push herself up, but she whimpered and slumped down again as new agonies ripped through her insides.

The other slaves stood where they were, afraid to move until the whites were out of view. When Ambrose Maxwell and his two henchmen could no longer be seen, the slaves went about their business. Only a few—including Batteau and Jacques—went to assist Eve. As they helped her to her feet, Maxwell heard growling. He turned to see two of the master's hounds snarling at each other as they wolfed down Toby's sex organs. The one-time house slave was still alive and was weakly trying to crawl away from the animals. He didn't get far before the dogs, now with the scent of blood in their nostrils and the taste of it on their tongues, attacked Toby. He was too weak to scream.

Batteau and Maxwell got Eve into the shack they

shared with more than a dozen other slaves, and set her down. One of the older women took over. Assisted by several other women, she treated Eve as best she could with what she had at hand.

Eve lived after the severe beating she had undergone, though she lost the child, of course.

Maxwell was glad of that, overjoyed at first, until he began to notice that his mother was no longer the same woman she had been. Despite the wretchedness of the slaves' existence, Eve had always been cheerful. She had always tried to smile at her companions, hoping to bring even the smallest ray of sunshine into their dismal, hopeless lives. But no longer. She did everything with her head bowed, as if in shame, and a grim face.

It took Maxwell, as young as he yet was, a while to realize just why his mother did that. He learned through circuitous ways that many of the slaves wanted no part of Eve. Some blamed her for the even more harsh treatment they had been receiving since that day. While few of the slaves outside the house had cared much for Toby, they found it difficult to accept that Eve had so callously offered him up for a sacrifice. They could not see that she knew Ambrose Maxwell far better than they did, and she could reason out what he would do.

That hurt Maxwell almost as much as the beating his mother had received, and he brooded about it, though there was nothing he could do, and he knew it. He went about picking cotton and doing anything else the white masters required, and kept his mouth quiet all the time, trying to ignore the humiliations he endured every minute of his life.

Eve lingered on almost two years, but by then the brutality of her existence became too much for her to bear. Maxwell awoke one morning with the harsh crowing of the cocks, and found that Eve had died during the night. The young man had no tears then. He had known it was coming, and he managed to bottle up whatever emotions wanted to get out. They had no place here.

Maxwell, the two of his brothers who had not been sold off, and Batteau buried Eve in the sere patch of ground used for slave burials. Another slave shack had once stood on the ground, but when some of the slaves asked for a cemetery, Ambrose had it razed and moved those residents into the other, already overcrowded shacks.

Afterward, one of Maxwell's sisters—Esmerelda—went to the main house to tell the master that Eve had died. She was less than five minutes behind the rest of the slaves who were already at work in the fields.

The next day, Ambrose showed up at Maxwell's shack just before dark. Without a word of any kind, he took twelve-year-old Esmerelda with him.

Batteau had to use his considerable size and strength to hold Maxwell back from attacking his father. "That will only bring more trouble, son," Batteau said in French. "You know that."

"I don't care," Maxwell hissed, also in French. "I will kill him."

"*Mais non,*" Batteau said roughly, still in French. "That won't do."

"But . . . "

"It would only get you killed and bring trouble on the others here," Batteau insisted. "If you want to do something, do something for yourself."

Maxwell looked at him, eyes narrowed as he tried to puzzle out what Batteau was telling him. Then he nodded, knowing what he must do.

It took Maxwell some months to prepare, but then he was ready. Without a word to anyone—lest they get in trouble for aiding him—sixteen-year-old Maxwell slipped out of his shack one night. He headed he knew not where, using the moonlight to see by. He moved as fast as he dared, wanting to get as far away from Falling Oaks as he could before the sun rose.

8

Maxwell had only the vaguest notion of where he was, and no idea of where he was going, or even where he should go. He managed to get to the banks of the Atchafalaya River and started following it. He went north at first, figuring that safety lay that way. But a natural cunning and a good instinct made him swing around a hundred and eighty degrees and head southward. He hoped his master, the overseers, and the bounty hunters would all figure he went north.

He traveled as steadily as he could, while fighting through dank, dangerous swamps, which filled Maxwell's superstitious heart with dread, where the sounds and smells conspired to terrify him so much that he considered with frightening regularity returning to Falling Oaks, Ambrose Maxwell's plantation near the small town of Plaquemine. But each time he thought of doing such an unthinkable thing, he would remember his mother, Eve, battered and broken on the ground. And he would remember the house slave, Toby, dead in the dirt, his genitals being gobbled down by Ambrose's dogs. With such pictures so vividly clear in his mind, all thought of returning to Falling Oaks was forgotten. The horrors there far, far outweighed the terrors of the numerous reeking swamps.

There were plenty of impediments on his way to freedom. Numerous streams flowed into the Atchafalaya River, and he had to splash across them, hoping he wouldn't lose the river in the doing. He did, though, several times, and had to retrace his steps until he was back on the proper track.

And he had no food. He was loath to steal, but he soon had no other choice. He knew, however, that each time he made a foray into some farmhouse, or slipped into a town under the cover of darkness to steal a loaf of bread, some fruit, or a bit of salted meat, he ran a great risk of discovery. And, if found, he would be returned to Falling Oaks as quickly as possible. There, of course, he would face a most terrible punishment. Though he could think of none worse than Toby had undergone, he feared that his father would come up with something even more devilish for him. It was not a thought he wanted to contemplate, so he kept his food-stealing raids to a minimum. He found early on that he could catch plenty of crawfish with little effort. They were not big, and he had to catch a mess of them to make even a halfway decent meal, but he did it. He rigged up a makeshift fishing line and hook, and caught fish—he found that he liked catfish particularly. He had to make fires to cook his catches, though he feared the smoke would give him away. Sometimes he managed to trap rats—repulsive to eat, but at times they were all he had, and they would keep him alive.

The darkness held its own terrors. There were strange sounds and odd smells, and he sometimes was forced to sleep in a tree, or in a hastily scooped-out hole in the riverbank, or on tufts of grass on swampy ground.

With those terrors came the added dread of animals—huge, hungry alligators with man-crunching jaws; white-fanged, cagey pumas and wildcats; snapping turtles; and creatures Maxwell did not know and would rather not even think about. Especially the snakes, the poisonous vipers that skimmed through the rank water of the swamps, and the others that waited on the land. Maxwell learned very quickly that he dreaded serpents.

Perhaps the worst, though, was the loneliness. As bad as things had been back at Falling Oaks, he had always been around people. His own people. This was the first time he could remember that he was utterly alone. There was no Eve to watch over him even the little bit she had been allowed to; no Henri Batteau to act as a father; no people he knew well, and who were in the same wretched position as he was. The solitude gave him too much time to think, too much time to remember all that he had lost. At times, he wanted to just sit and cry, and perhaps die, so that he would no longer have to endure this life of misery.

But he forced himself to push on, avoiding towns almost entirely, choosing to raid isolated farms and cabins for provisions, thinking that far less likely to lead to his detection. He also tried to avoid all travelers, even other slaves. Whenever he heard someone coming, he would dash into the brush, or up a tree, or even into the fast-moving river, whatever was handiest to hide him from the eyes of anyone who might turn him in.

Despite all his efforts at escaping detection, Maxwell could not avoid one encounter, and he could have hardly envisioned a worse confrontation.

He was sleeping in some rushes when the sound of dried vegetation crunching under someone's foot woke him. Then he heard the excited yelping of a dog. Panicking, Maxwell's first thought was to jump up and run like hell; his second was to just stay where he was and hope he would not be discovered. Then he realized that neither idea was any good. Staying would not delay his discovery for very long, since the dog was sure to find him. Running would just allow whoever was out there to follow him more easily.

His heart pounded as he pondered what to do. He felt the hilt of the stolen knife jabbing him in the side. *Would that be of any use?* he wondered. He doubted it, since he had never used a weapon against another. Still, it reassured him just a little to know it was there.

Maxwell's decision was made for him when a hound suddenly bounded up and began baying loudly, right in his face. Fearing that the animal— one of his father's, he was certain—would suddenly start to tear at him, Maxwell whipped out his knife and without thought slashed the dog's throat. The dog yelped loudly once, then gurgled a bit, wobbled off a few steps, and fell, still making horrible dying noises that unsettled Maxwell no end.

Maxwell scuttled off, rattling the rushes a little, but not as badly as he had feared. He breathed a sigh of relief, thinking that perhaps he could move slowly away from the spot without making too much noise or leaving much of a trail. He hoped it would help him avoid detection by the man who was on his trail. He managed to get perhaps twenty yards ahead when he heard the footsteps getting near the spot where he had slain the dog. He stopped and lay quietly, sweat streaming down his handsome, dark-tan face.

For a long time he lay there, even after he could hear no more footsteps. He wanted to be absolutely sure that whoever was tracking him was gone.

So it came as an incredible surprise when a lash whipped painfully across his side and back. "Thought you'd gotten away, did you, you damn fool nigger?" a harsh voice asked. "Ain't likely with Papa Beaulieu trailin' yo' black ass."

The lash came down again. When it cut into Maxwell's flesh, it galvanized him into action. The slave rolled out of the way and uneasily rose to his feet. He tried to ignore the sting where the whip had cut across him twice. He knew that he was in great trouble. Papa Beaulieu was the most feared tracker of runaway slaves in the region. He was usually hired by slave owners who had a special reason for having a runaway tracked down and killed, since Papa Beaulieu refused to return a living slave—unless he had the personal assurance of the slave owner that the runaway would be suitably tortured in his presence before being killed.

Maxwell was paralyzed with terror. Papa Beaulieu was a big man, and one, word had it, without remorse for the killing of people, whether slave or white. He was heartless, perhaps even soulless, which meant to Maxwell that he probably could not be beaten or killed. Beaulieu was a man above all that, perhaps not even a man at all, but some form of spirit sent to earth to visit terror on the countryside with the sole purpose of keeping slaves—and their masters—in line. Or so Maxwell believed. It was the only thing he could believe.

"I'm a mind to kilt you right here, boy," Beaulieu said in that flat, unearthly tone that was his way. "But yo' master wants yo' black ass alive, boy." He grinned icily. "I expect 'e 'ave somet'ing special to done to you first before 'e tosses you in the fire."

"Please, *Maître* Beaulieu," Maxwell heard himself pleading. He fell to his knees in supplication. "Please don' take me back zere. Please."

"Got up, you sniveling black bastard," Beaulieu said with a sneer. It was usually this way. As if the pleadings of some runaway black would have any influence on him. It was a pitiful thing to see. Or at least it would be pitiful if these creatures had any humanity about them.

"But *maître* . . . "

"Got up, you stinking black animal," Beaulieu hissed, getting angry. "I got no time for dis here nonsense." He lashed out again, and the end of the whip cracked painfully on Maxwell's cheekbone. Then again. "Did as I say, damn insolent nigger."

As Beaulieu reached back to lash out with the whip again, something inside of Maxwell snapped. In less than a heartbeat, he relived that day his father beat his mother worse than he ever would his dogs, and how he had so callously let his overseers slice off Toby's essence and then let him die in the dirt while the dogs gnawed on what had made the house slave a man. And before the leather of the whip could split his flesh again, Maxwell had decided that he would not go back to such a life—and such a horrible death. He would rather die here and now, trying to be free, than live even a few more days only to face unmentionable torture at the hands of Ambrose Maxwell.

Without really knowing that he was reacting, Maxwell reached out and grabbed the sizzling strand of the whip and managed to get it wrapped around his left arm a little. He ignored the new pains that flashed through his arm flesh, as he jerked Beaulieu toward him with the whip.

The slave tracker was startled. Not since his first days as a bounty man had Beaulieu met such resistance. His reputation was enough to keep these runaway slaves the obedient creatures they were supposed to be. Now this. He was insulted, enraged. He tried to resist the pull of the whip, but could not, so he let the whip handle go. But he had forgotten that it was still attached to the loop wrapped around his wrist. He could not worry about that now, though. He had to do something, and mighty fast. He hastily reached for the single-shot flintlock pistol stuck in his waistband.

Maxwell almost fell off balance when Beaulieu let go of the whip handle, but then the thong on

Beaulieu's wrist caught, and Maxwell began tugging again. The slave had no real idea of what he was going to do. All he wanted was to end this threat and to escape the tracker's clutches, even if it meant dying, which was likely. So he reacted without thinking, really, pulling the slave hunter toward him with an unyielding pressure. His eyes saw Beaulieu reach for his gun, and the information registered in his brain.

Almost instinctively, Maxwell dropped his small sack of belongings and pulled the knife from the rope he wore as a belt. The blade was still stickily wet with the dog's blood. Maxwell gave one final mighty jerk on the whip. Beaulieu stumbled forward, and just before the two men hit, Maxwell managed to plunge his knife deep into the slave hunter's stomach.

Beaulieu's dark eyes registered a considerable amount of amazement as the knife sliced into him. He made another effort to reach the pistol in his waistband, but his hands and arms were not working properly. He could not understand it. Still, he did manage to get the pistol out, but before he could cock it, Maxwell had plunged the knife into his belly again and then into his chest.

Beaulieu groaned as the shock of his injuries hit him. He dropped the pistol and sagged against Maxwell, his nose recoiling from the slave's offensive odor even as his life drained from him. He could not smell his own fear, or the stench that came when his bowels released their contents through a suddenly nonworking sphincter.

Maxwell pushed the dying man away from him and looked down at the soon-to-be-corpse. He felt a mixture of shame and fear, relief and regret. He knew he had done what he had to do, but he had never killed a man before, and he was not at all sure he liked the idea of being responsible for taking a man's life.

His first thought was to run as far and as fast as he could. But he held himself in check. He heard no one else in the vicinity, and it was evident that there were no other dogs around. He gathered up his few little things, wiped the knife on Beaulieu's shirt, and then went through the slave hunter's clothing. He found twelve dollars—more money than he had ever seen in his lifetime, probably more than all the slaves at Falling Oaks had put together. He slipped the pouch of coins onto his rope belt. He wondered whether to take Beaulieu's pistol, and then decided he would. Though he did not know how to use it, he figured he could learn quickly enough. He had seen his father and the overseers fire and load their guns, but Maxwell had never done it himself. He would study it when he had the time. He also took the powder flask and pouch of lead balls that Beaulieu had carried.

Maxwell also found some tobacco and a pipe, which he took. He decided that he would try them one day soon. He left the whip, but took the long, thin, deadly-looking dagger that the slave hunter carried with him.

With panic growing inside him again, Maxwell finally decided it was time to leave. He had to get away from this spot, and quickly. Grabbing his little canvas sack, he took off, moving swiftly toward the river some yards to his left. He walked carefully across the river, almost drowning at one point when the current swept his feet out from under him. Then he regained his footing and made it to the other side, but the hard-won gun was lost downstream. He walked as fast as he could, weaving between thickets and clumps of brush, which served to protect him at least somewhat from detection.

A mile on, he found a good spot and recrossed the river, hoping to throw off any pursuers that might come along. He did that again, and yet again during the day.

By dark, he figured he had put ten miles behind him. He did not believe he was perfectly safe yet, and he still felt considerably guilty about having killed a white man, but he knew he had to stop, at least for the night. With the darkness quickly closing in on him, Maxwell waded to a small island in the midst of another swamp. Exhausted, he curled up on some grass, hoping that the 'gators, snakes, and mosquitoes would leave him alone. He was asleep in moments, though his dreams that night were filled with horrifying scenes of dead men and dead animals rising from the earth to chase him. He awoke twice, shaking from the vivid, terrifying images.

9

Maxwell continued moving quickly but warily, watching for people of any color. He didn't want to see anyone. But as he neared the Gulf Coast, it became more and more difficult. At one point, he actually stumbled into a small camp.

The occupants were whites, a family, Maxwell assumed. There was a man, a woman, and three scruffy kids. They were clearly of the poorest class of whites, though it was obvious with one look that they still considered themselves far superior to Maxwell.

"You got any food in that sack there, boy?" the man asked, rising from the stump on which he had been sitting.

"*Mais non, maître,*" Maxwell mumbled in his best slave voice, despite the surge of anger he felt.

"Well, let me see that sack anyway, boy," the man commanded. "Jus' to make sho'."

"I said I got none, massah," Maxwell insisted. He did not feel the least bit guilty in lying.

"And I said I aim to look. Even if you got no

food in there, damn your black hide, you might have somethin' else I can make use of." His drawl was thick, like cold molasses oozing down the bark of a tree. He moved toward Maxwell.

"Don' came no closer, massah," Maxwell warned, holding out one hand, palm outward.

The man stopped, surprised. "What'd you say to me, boy?" the man asked, his voice harsh with anger and affront.

"You heard me, *monsieur*," Maxwell said. He was still scared, having never even considered doing something like this before. Since the day he had been born he had been trained to be obsequious to whites. Any whites. All whites. Simply talking back to even the poorest of them, as he was doing now, went against everything he had been taught. Yes, he had killed a white man not long ago, but that had been a different circumstance. That had been propelled by the absolute fear of knowing what faced him at the hands of the man who had tracked him down. He was simply trying to protect himself, and what had transpired was instinctual, more or less. But this was plainly defiance on his part. Out and out rebellion, and it ate at him even as he did it so calmly.

"You're one impudent black bastard, ain't you, boy?" the man questioned, his eyes blazing with hatred.

"*Mais non, monsieur*. But I won' let you seen what's in my sack 'ere."

"What you hidin' in there, boy?"

"Not'ing, *monsieur*."

"I think you're a lyin' bastard, boy. Now give me over that sack there, before I take a whip to you."

"You do zat, *monsieur*, and I'll 'ave to kill you."

"You insolent son of a bitch," the man said. He was livid. He advanced, hand raised. He was too poor to actually have a whip, and he was too angry to think of any other weapon to grab. Still, he was not concerned. He could attack this slave with impunity and without fear.

Still afraid that he was going against the natural order of the world, Maxwell quickly stepped up and slammed a fist into the man's face. Startled, the man fell onto his rump.

"Don' try to 'urt me again, *monsieur*," Maxwell said. "I don' want to 'urt you. I come 'ere by mistake. I jus' want to go away wit'out 'aving any trouble. Zat's all."

"Like hell you're goin' anywhere, boy," the man said, rising and swatting dirt from the back of his pants. "Ain't no goddamn darky puts a hand on me and gits away with it."

"*Monsieur*," Maxwell said wearily, his natural perceptiveness rising to guide him, "I 'ave not'ing to lose, so I can fight you wit' no worries, *n'est-ce pas?* But you, you ave a family 'ere who you should t'ink about."

The man spit. He scanned his simple camp, until he spied his hatchet, stuck into a fallen log. That was all he had in the way of a weapon, but it would do just fine, he figured. He pulled it out of the wood, and moved toward Maxwell.

The slave became frightened again. Not scared of being killed; that was of little consequence to him. No, he was apprehensive because he was once again going to act counter to everything he had ever learned, and fight with a white man. If he allowed it, the conflict between training and action might tear him apart mentally, but in the few weeks since he had run away from Falling Oaks, he had grown within himself. He had begun to sense what independence could be, and he was starting to learn that he did not have to act the way he had been taught all his life. He could be a free man. But still, sixteen years of indoctrination in slave behavior was not all that easy to wipe away in a few weeks.

Maxwell waited, fear and anxiety tickling his intestines, making him want to urinate. But he tried as hard as he could to keep a calm demeanor. Suddenly he flung his sack at the man, who ducked. Maxwell used the opportunity to hit him several times, and then kick the hatchet out of his hand. As the man rose again, more angry than ever, Maxwell scooped up a hefty piece of wood and slammed it against the side of the man's head.

The man fell and lay still. Maxwell knelt next to him, and could see that his chest rose and fell regularly and that the big artery in his neck beat steadily. Maxwell rose and retrieved his sack. All he wanted was to get away. He glanced at the woman and the three children. They were huddled together on the far side of the measly fire. All looked frightened to death, and he knew without doubt that they were terrified of him.

Maxwell began to leave, but then stopped and turned back. He went toward where the four family members clustered, and he knelt next to them. "I won' 'urt you," he said quietly. His words had no effect on the people. Still kneeling, Maxwell took another look around the camp There was an iron pot dangling over the small fire. Maxwell arose and walked to it. There was some kind of soup in it, but even to the slave, who was used to the worst possible food, this did not look very tasty nor very nourishing. It was, however, the only food he saw in the forlorn little camp.

With a sigh, he reached into his sack and pulled out the small rag-wrapped chunk of salted meat and a little calico pouch of turnips he had found just the other day. He laid the two items on a rock next to the fire and then looked over his shoulder at the woman. "For ze children," he said lamely. Then he trotted off into the cover of the bushes.

He moved swiftly for a while, wanting to get as far away from the little camp as he could. He had seen no one else in the area, but still, he could not be sure that the man wouldn't wake up and know of somewhere nearby to go to get help.

As he moved, Maxwell worried about running into another group of whites. But he could not concern himself about that too much. This encounter was purely happenstance; he did not think it likely to occur again.

It took another month, but Maxwell finally made his way down to the Gulf of Mexico. He sat at an isolated place, looking out over the vast expanse of rippling water, and wondered what he should do. He knew he could not stay where he was, since it was a virtual certainty that he would be discovered, and probably soon.

What was worse, he had only a vague notion of what lay in any other direction. He knew, obviously, that heading north from here was not wise, as it would take him back toward Falling Oaks and his father. But he knew not what lay to the east and west. He had heard tales that another country lay not too far to the west, and all the talk was that there were more plantations and more slavery to the east.

It didn't take long for Maxwell to decide that west was the only way for him to go. He could not take the chance of encountering another region as heavily populated by plantations and slavery as this one. He would rather risk entering a foreign country.

He was finding it easier to steal, having done it often enough. However, he tried to steal only from whites, even the poorest of them. He would not allow himself to steal from blacks, even if they were free men. He just would not do it.

So he made his way to a nearby town, and when darkness covered his actions, he slipped in, broke into a store through the back entrance, and filled a sack with salted meat, bacon, cornmeal, a shirt, a pair of pants, boots, tea, a full canteen, small pot and pan, a cup, and a fire-starting kit, including charred cloth. He made his way carefully out of the town, and then hurried away. He returned to the small haven he had found in the midst of a thicket, just off a sandy beach touching a rough little cove. There he tossed away the rags he had been wearing since leaving Falling Oaks and put on the first set of real clothes he had ever owned—the clothes of a free man.

Maxwell wanted to build a fire to cook some of

the food he had taken, but common sense prevailed and he decided to wait, despite the hunger growls emanating from his belly.

In the morning, he took a good look around as he gathered some firewood. Having seen nothing out of the ordinary, he eagerly built a fire. That small act, however, took a considerable amount of time. For some reason the tinder did not want to catch. He chopped at the slim hunk of flint with the curled piece of steel. Sparks sputtered and flew, but none seemed to take the notion to catch on to the charred cloth and set it to burning. Considerably hungry now, Maxwell was getting mighty frustrated from his failure to get a fire started.

Finally he got so angry that he rose and stormed out of the thicket, cursing and hollering up a storm. He stomped around the beach, kicking up sand, calling himself all manner of names. Suddenly he thought he heard something. He stopped and looked around. He could see nothing, but he was sure someone was coming. He was a lot closer to the gulf than he was to the safety of his thicket, so he charged into the surf, waded out a little ways, and then ducked under the water. He sat and watched the shore, waiting for someone to come by. After what seemed a long time, no one appeared, and he assumed he had just imagined he had heard something. And he realized that his temper had cooled while sitting there in the water.

With a small smile, he rose and waded out of the water. He stood there a few minutes, letting the wind dry him off. In a better frame of mind, he headed back into his thicket. Despite still being damp, he had little trouble creating a fire this time. He believed that was because he had found his way back into Simbi's graces. The god of watery places must have taken a liking to him when he squatted in the gulf, he thought.

He cooked up more food than he thought he needed, but he couldn't help it. When it came to eating, though, it wasn't quite enough to fill his belly. Still, it was a good deal better than he had ever had. His breakfast topped off with two cups of hot, tart tea, Maxwell felt as if he could go on forever.

So content was he after the repast, that he almost felt like staying here a while. It was quiet, there was good water from a little spring that bubbled several yards behind him, and there seemed to be no one in the vicinity. In addition, the town—too small to even have a name—was close enough to keep him supplied with food.

But he knew that staying here would be foolhardy, and his sense finally overrode his desire for comfort. He packed his few personal items in the sack, stuck his stolen knife into his rope belt, and marched out, heading west.

For the next two years, Maxwell followed the rough, jagged coastline west and southwest. For a long while, he continued to avoid people, certain that anyone who saw him would kill him or capture him and return him to his master. But he knew that eventually he had to stop doing that. He could not continue stealing food from stores and farmhouses. And he had to mingle with people sooner or later.

It took him almost a year, but he finally walked into a town. It was a polyglot kind of place, with people of all hues. No one seemed to look oddly at him or question him just for arriving.

After that it became easier, though some places were much more open to strangers than others. He quickly became adept at distinguishing the character of a place right off, and conducted himself accordingly.

Soon, he would stop and visit any place that looked as if it had something of interest, whether it was work for some cash he could use to buy food, drink, or other needs. Or it might be that he wanted a woman. He made stops at pirate havens, small islands used by smugglers just off the coast, and little settlements of freed or escaped slaves hidden among the brush and trees. He even, on occasion, stopped in slave-trading towns, walking bravely down the streets as if he owned them. No one bothered him, thinking he was a free man. It gave him a delicious thrill to do that. The danger-tinged atmosphere was something he had quickly come to enjoy.

He also learned to like battle, the fights that he encountered everywhere he went. He survived numerous scrapes, though not always without some damage. But in the process he became a tough, fearless young man. In some ways he was even cocky, but it was a well-deserved arrogance.

One day, almost two years after running away from his father at Falling Oaks, Maxwell was in a rancid saloon on the coast, well south of where the gulf made its giant, sweeping curve. The saloon had no name, and Maxwell was not even sure that the town had one. Not that it mattered to him or anyone else who showed up in such a place.

Maxwell had pulled in only this morning. He was shoveling down food and drink, having learned to like a wide variety of both. He planned to eat and then find himself a woman for the night. That shouldn't be too difficult in a place like this; he had already spotted several women plying their trade in the fetid saloon. One of them even was mildly attractive. He had set his sights on her.

But before he could finish his meal, several vicious-looking pirates began making fun of him, criticizing his eating habits, his looks, and his parentage. Most of it he did not mind, but when they began on his lineage, he took exception.

10

Maxwell calmly finished his meal, wiped a sleeve across his greasy lips, had one last swallow of whiskey, and then stood.

"You boys 'ave said enough, *n'est-ce pas?*" Maxwell said evenly. "Maybe you 'ave mothers who are whores and nagging shrews, eh, but zat is your problem. *Mais oui.* It does not gave you ze right to said bad t'ings about *ma mere. Non, non.*"

"So, you're still tied to your mama's apron strings, is 'at it?" one of the pirates rasped.

Maxwell shrugged. "If zat means do I love *ma mere?* Zen ze answer is *mais oui.* If you mean somet'ing else, zen I said ze answer is no."

"You're mighty insolent, boy, for a slave," another snapped.

"I am no slave, *monsieur,*" Maxwell said with dignity.

"You ain't no freed man, boy," the first pirate said. "You got the look of a runaway about you."

"And there are many folks who'll pay top

money for the return of runaway slaves, boy," the second added.

Maxwell pushed his wood chair out of the way and stepped around the table. "Is zat your plan, *monsieurs?*" he asked, seemingly unconcerned.

"Jus' might be," the first one said. He pulled out a knife and ran a thumb along the edge of it.

"Zen zere is no more need to parley, eh?" Maxwell said, and he kicked the first pirate in the side. As the pirate doubled over with several broken ribs, Maxwell slammed his locked fists down on the back of the man's neck. He fell, and Maxwell turned to face the others.

The four pirates piled on him, dragging him to the ground. They thought it would be easy once they got Maxwell down, but they had not counted on facing a wild man. That's what they had on their hands. To the four pirates, it seemed as if Maxwell had ten arms and ten legs. The former slave's elbows, feet, and fists seemed to be everywhere, anywhere the pirates tried to land a punch or gain an advantage. Teeth flew about, and blood droplets were sprayed around as cuts opened up on all the combatants.

Maxwell wriggled and slithered, managing to continually slide out of the pirates' grasp, until his four foes began to think they were trying to hold down a giant eel. Maxwell jammed a thumb into one pirate's eye, and cracked another's rib with an elbow. A ragged fingernail tore a jagged slice in one foe's flesh, and Maxwell's teeth ripped a chunk out of someone's arm.

It took a while, but somehow Maxwell regained

his footing. Standing, he had much more mobility and a much larger choice of weapons. He made use of them, too, while fending off most of his opponents' attacks.

With crushing efficiency, Maxwell grabbed a hardwood chair and smashed it into a pirate's chest as the man charged toward him with a knife in his hand. When someone pounded Maxwell on the back of the head with a fist, he lost control of the chair and it went spinning and crashing away from him. He ducked under a table and came up on the other side, grabbing a whiskey bottle, which he promptly slammed into another foe's face.

There were only two of the pirates standing now, and both had more damage to them than Maxwell did. At this point, Maxwell was not about to give them any quarter. He did not plan to kill them, but he did aim to see that they joined their companions in unconsciousness. But as Maxwell advanced on them, both turned and ran for the door. As battered as he was, Maxwell gave chase, and caught one. He jumped on the man's back, driving him to the floor.

"I'll taught you to say bad t'ings about *ma mere, espèce* ze *merde*—you shit," Maxwell growled, kneeling on the man's back. He grabbed the pirate's scraggly hair, lifted his head, then slammed his foe's face onto the floor. He did that several times until the pirate gave up any show of consciousness.

Maxwell rose and looked around the room. Several tables and even more chairs were overturned and lay haphazardly around the room. There were a couple of broken bottles and glasses, but many more just rolled around, still spitting out small streams of liquid. No one else seemed interested in bothering him.

With a nod, Maxwell returned to his table, which was lying on its side, as was his chair. He righted both, and called for another bottle of whiskey and a glass. Both were quickly brought to him by a frightened-looking black bartender. Maxwell sat and poured himself a drink. He downed a fair portion of it, letting its heat and fire spread through the inside of his body.

Then he began looking at his wounds. None that he could see was bad. He had a broken or disjointed finger, a number of scrapes, small cuts here and there, and he knew his face was already beginning to puff up with bruises. He hoped he didn't look too hideous, for he had also acquired a fair amount of vanity in his travels. Still, his desire to spend a night with a woman had dimmed somewhat since his little melee. He figured such an activity could wait a day or two.

Maxwell called for another bowl of the poor seafood gumbo, and sat eating it, trying to hide the winces that came involuntarily when the hot soup hit tender spots inside his mouth. He had bitten his cheek at least once during the fight, and it was sore.

He was still downing the food a short time later when a dashing, jovially fierce-looking fellow came into the saloon, followed by a group of men who looked like the ones Maxwell had fought earlier. The dashing man stopped, and one of his followers pointed to Maxwell, and whispered in the man's ear.

The man—obviously the leader of this group—nodded and headed straight for Maxwell's table.

He stopped at the table, picked up an overturned chair, set it right, and then sat. A moment later, the bartender appeared as if by magic, and set down a bottle of good wine and two relatively clean glasses. The newcomer filled the crockery glasses and pushed one across the table to Maxwell. Then he raised his own and held it out as a sort of toast.

Maxwell sat there, making no effort to pick up the glass of wine. He knew instinctively that the five men he had thrashed had worked for this man. Because of that, he was certain he was about to die, but he vowed then and there to take out as many of the pirates as he could before he went down. He was wary of the leader—and the offer of good wine.

After a sip of the wine, the man set the glass down and said, "*Je m'appelle* Jean Lafitte."

Maxwell was shocked. Like everyone else in these parts, he had heard plenty about the pirate captain. He was in for an even greater surprise with Lafitte's next words.

"I'd like you to join my crew, *monsieur*. Indeed, it would be a great honor to me to 'ave you serve *avec moi*."

Maxwell hesitated, uncertain. He worried that he was about to be made a fool of, or about to be taken advantage of. There could be no reason for a man such as Jean Lafitte to want him to be a member of his crew. Maxwell was pretty sure that if he agreed to this, Lafitte would simply make him a slave, only this time aboard a ship, where he couldn't escape.

Seeing Maxwell's indecision, Lafitte said, "Any man who can thrash four or five of me hardest men all by himself *should* be a member of my crew, *n'est-ce pas?*"

Maxwell was still unsure. While the sense of adventure appealed to him, he still could not rid himself of the thought that he was to be made only a slave.

"Take a look around you, *monsieur*," Lafitte said. "Look at my men. Zey are all ze same, *ça va?*"

Maxwell did look around. He noticed that while most of the men were French or Cajun, there were also a few blacks, some Spaniards, and what might have been an Indian or two. "I won' be made a slave on your ship, *Monsieur le Capitaine?*" he asked, skeptically.

"Mais non!" Lafitte said expansively. "Why would I take such a grand fighting man as you and turn you into a galley slave, eh? Zat don' make sense, *ça va?*"

"I suppose not, *monsieur*." Maxwell thought about it a moment, then asked, "But what about ze others?"

"What others?" Lafitte asked, surprised. He took another sip of wine.

"De ones I kicked around before."

"What about zem?"

"Won' zey be against me?" Maxwell asked. "Won' zey have trouble wit' me if I am one of your crewmen?"

Lafitte shrugged. "Zat is for zem to work out, *ça va?* Zey know zat if zey come at you in ze night, or try to stab you in ze back, I will dump zem in ze gulf to drown or be eaten by ze sharks. If zey want to challenge you face to your face, zen you will 'ave to do zat."

"I t'ink I showed I can did zat."

"*Mais oui*, zat you did!" Lafitte agreed. "So, what do you say, *monsieur*? Will you join us?"

After only a few more moments' thought, Maxwell agreed. He could see the hard look in Lafitte's eyes, and from that knew he really had little choice. Besides, there was the adventure such a life meant. He would have money from all the booty they would collect, and so he could have his choice of women, and he could eat and drink well, and perhaps someday rise to where he might even command a ship of his own.

He smiled at his foolishness. His thoughts were far too grandiose. Still, there should be excitement galore if he joined the crew of the great pirate Jean Lafitte.

"*Oui*, I will do it, *Monsieur le Capitaine*."

"*Bon*," Lafitte said loudly, letting the world know of his approval of this act. "Now, *monsieur*, we shall drink to our agreement, eh?"

It was not really a question, and Maxwell knew it. He lifted his glass in a little toast, then drank down the full glass of wine.

Lafitte also did so, then stood. "Well, *monsieur*," he said, then stopped. "But what is your name?"

"*Je m'appelle* Jacques Maxwell."

"Well zen, *Monsieur* Maxwell," Lafitte said with a nod, "now you are one of us. 'Ave you evair worked on a ship before?"

"*Mais non*," Maxwell said, suddenly growing sad. He figured for sure now that Lafitte would want nothing to do with him.

"No matter. Many of ze men learned while zey were doing it. You will do ze same, *ça va?*" Lafitte did not wait for an answer. "We set sail in two days. I will send one of my men for you tomorrow. Until zen, enjoy your time on land, *mon ami*. It may be quite a while before you get ashore again. You may 'ave ze wine zere on your table. My compliments, *monsieur*. Now, *a bientot*."

"*Au 'voir, Monsieur le Capitaine*." Maxwell watched as Lafitte and his men walked out of the saloon. He was still amazed at all that had transpired in less than an hour. He began to think that perhaps he had really gotten kicked in the head during the fight and was imagining all this. Regardless, if he still had this vision tomorrow night, he would go along with whatever crewman Lafitte sent to fetch him.

For this night, however, his mind returned to his original plan—to have a woman. If he was going to be out at sea for any length of time, he would need to take care of his baser needs enough to last him a while. He no longer cared that he ached in many spots, and that his face and knuckles were puffed up from the fight. The fine wine Lafitte had left for him would ease a lot of his pains; a woman would soothe the rest.

It was not long before he took his bottle, and the backpack he had made himself of wood, canvas, and rope, and headed to a small shack out back of the saloon with a willing wench named Juanita. Maxwell was mighty low on cash, but he didn't much care. He would soon be aboard ship, and thus have no place to spend any money. And, if he were still alive when he returned to shore, he should have plenty of cash to fling about. Right now, however, he wanted a good spree before he took this plunge into pirating.

He paid to spend the night with Juanita, handing the money over to the bartender before being led out to the shack in back. It took her only moments to divest herself of her simple garments, and then she lay on the bed, waiting for him, a bored expression on her face.

"You might at least pretend a bit zat you enjoy what we'll do, *mademoiselle*," Maxwell said with a small smile. "Wit' all ze money I paid for you . . . "

Juanita smiled just a little. She was not against enjoying herself in such situations. Maxwell was a handsome enough young man, she figured, even though his face was now disfigured with swelling. She became more intrigued when Maxwell shucked his clothes. She quickly learned that he was not innocent of women.

And, of course, he was still young enough to be randy nearly all the time.

He figured in the morning that the money he had paid for the night with Juanita was well worth it. Yes, she had been much to thin for his tastes, and she was missing a few too many teeth for one so young. But once she had learned that he knew what he was doing to some extent, she had become a much more willing participant, making up in enthusiasm and enjoyment what she might have lacked in beauty and figure.

Maxwell had just about enough money left over for one good meal and, just before being called to the ship, a poor one. He spent the day resting in the shade of a building, trying to let his body heal.

As he lay there, he again began to have some misgivings about what he had agreed to do. He knew nothing of the sea, and was not certain he wanted to. Looking out across that vast expanse of water had always filled him with a fair amount of dread. It seemed so unnatural to him to take a wooden boat and go sailing out across that endless emptiness, at the hands of the weather. He could not swim. What would happen to him if he were thrown overboard? What would happen if he got sea sick? He had heard that many people were like that. There were so many potential problems and terrors that he was soon regretting what he had promised.

After a nap, however, he woke to realize that while many of his concerns were real, he was still excited about the possibilities for making a fortune and for having the adventure of a lifetime. For a young man who had been a slave barely two years ago, the dangers of the sea were too small to worry about.

For the next few years, Maxwell plundered the Gulf of Mexico with Lafitte, getting into adventures so numerous, at times he could not recall half of them. Along the way, he toughened himself even more. It was everything he hoped it would be—and then some. Sure, there were bad periods amid all the adventures, but the good times far outweighed the bad, at least as far as Maxwell was concerned.

Well, perhaps that hadn't been true the whole time.

There was, after all, the incident after Lafitte's swift, well-handled ship ran down a British frigate. As Lafitte's pirates scrambled aboard the vessel floating the Union Jack, Maxwell suddenly found himself face to face with a raving lunatic of a Scotsman. The Scot had lost an eye and a great many of his teeth. He apparently was missing much of his sense, too, Maxwell believed, since he charged in again and again on Maxwell, who was hacking away with his stolen cutlass.

Maxwell felt himself hard pressed, but

dispatched the Scotsman before too long. He had to fight the maniac so closely that he had no idea what else was going on around him. As he hacked the impressed British sailor to death with his cutlass, Maxwell stumbled a little, which was, he realized much later, what saved him from certain death, since another British seaman had taken a vicious cut at his head with a cutlass. The sword did not hit fully, or Maxwell would have gone down in a heap right away, but it did slice deeply into his left shoulder.

"*Un oeil qui dit nerde à l'autre balaise*—You cross-eyed hulking brute," Maxwell muttered. He shoved himself up on his feet, slipping a little in the dead Scotsman's blood. Heedless of his own blood flowing down his arm, Maxwell chopped the tall, stocky sailor to death with wild swings of his broad cutlass. The sailor was long dead and hacked to pieces when Maxwell fell atop him, unconscious, weakened by the loss of blood.

He came to in the hold of Lafitte's ship. Artemis Hines, who was nominally the ship's surgeon—only because he was more experienced than anyone else on the ship in cutting off rotten limbs and sewing up gaping wounds—was tending him.

"'Ow does it look, *Monsieur le* Doctor?" Maxwell asked nervously. He had never been injured this badly before. It hurt like hell, and he felt as weak as a newly hatched alligator.

"I've seen boys in worse shape than you, Jacques," Hines answered almost lightly. "Then again, old tar, I've seen men in a lot better condition than you are."

"You're not planning to took my arm, are you?"

Maxwell asked. He was frightened now. Since Hines was not really a doctor or a surgeon, he often sawed off a limb right away, figuring that it could not be saved. Maxwell was not about to let Hines do that to him so casually. Not yet, anyway.

"Ain't plannin' on it, no," Hines said easily. He knew what Maxwell was feeling, and he was well aware of his own reputation as a butcher because he was one of the few seamen here who had the courage to do those necessary things. "I'll just sew you up and send you on your way, ol' tar. You'll be like new in no time." He fully expected to see Maxwell again in a week or so, when he would have to chop off the pirate's infected, gangrenous arm. He shook his head. It had been easier when he was younger and would just do the amputation without hesitation or trepidation. But these days, he tried to soften the blow on the men somewhat. It really did not bother him to do so, and it seemed to make the crewmen handle such trying times a bit more easily.

"Well, zen, *mon ami*, start sewing," Maxwell said.

There were times over the next couple of weeks when Maxwell almost wished that Hines *had* amputated the arm. The pain was excruciating and unyielding. He either sat on deck, hoping the sea winds would cool his fever, or he lay belowdecks, rolling on his creaking little rope-and-blanket bunk while the pain coursed through his shoulder as if it were a part of his blood.

Sixteen days after being wounded, Maxwell sat up in the throes of the worst fever he had ever experienced. It was time, he thought. He would go to Hines and have the imitation surgeon cut the arm off and be done with it. He could not live with this agony and this raging temperature any longer. But he fell asleep again, thrashing about.

When he awoke, the desire to have his arm gone had disappeared. The fever had broken, and over the next several days he could feel himself beginning to mend. It was still some time before he got back his full vigor and strength in that arm, but it came to him.

By the time he felt pretty well healed, Maxwell was ready for some time on shore. He wanted something more than the grog served aboard ship, and he wanted a woman. The other men had partaken of such luxuries while Maxwell was recovering, so he was quite ready. But it was still some time before they pulled into port, on an island at the western curve of the Gulf of Mexico.

After a week of prowling the waterfront bars and bawdyhouses of Galveston Island—a mostly Spanish enclave named for the late Bernardo de Galvez, once the chief official for this whole area— Maxwell felt a discontent growing. He wasn't sure what the source of the unease was, so he tried to drown it with more grog, wine, and plain home-brewed whiskey. But the hangovers that accompanied such bouts of drunken foolishness only deepened the uneasiness he felt.

One morning, in the throes of another blistering hangover, as he hung his head out of the window of the shack he was temporarily calling home, he spotted a young woman sashaying past on the dusty little dirt road. Maxwell jerked his head up sharply, and instantly regretted it with every fiber of his being. His head pounded and roared, throbbed and shrunk. He lost his sight for a few moments as the agony seared through his nerves. He vomited, quickly turning into a shuddering, wretched caricature of a human being.

He finally thought himself ready to lift his head up a little, though he did so cautiously. Through bleary, bloodshot eyes, he saw the pretty young woman turn the corner around a building just down the street. Maxwell grimaced—it was the best he could do by way of a smile at the moment. Despite the crushing hangover, he knew what was wrong with him. It was as clear as the sweltering summer day.

Trouble was, now that he had his answer, he was absolutely incapable of doing anything about it at the moment. He drank another couple of gallons of water, or so it seemed to him, urinated, made crude noises from various orifices, and collapsed on the bed.

When he awoke twelve hours later, he felt considerably better. He was as hungry as a spring bear, though. He lurched outside, wondering what the offensive stench was, until he realized it was he who reeked. He shrugged. He could live with that for now. The first thing he had to do was eat.

That necessity was dispensed with quickly enough, and Maxwell felt nearly back to his normal self. He wondered what to do with himself. He was so used to spending all his time in saloons and other low dives, now that he did not want that he wasn't sure what to do. Slightly aggravated, he finally wandered down to the small town square.

The area was a mingling of French, Spanish, American, and other cultures. It was a place to relax and watch humanity pass by. Vendors sold various foods and craft items. There were slave sales at times, and the exchange of booty taken from Spanish, English, and American ships was a thriving activity. Beggars wandered amid the carts, horses and mules laden with loot, trying to cadge some *pesetas* or pieces of eight, or steal some fruit. Raucous children played here, as they did everywhere, with their mothers watching over them.

Maxwell took a seat on a log bench under a sprawling cypress, enjoying the shade. With the cool breeze thick with the smell of the salt sea, it was pleasant. As he watched the pass of humanity before him, Maxwell wondered what he should do now. The sight of that one young woman had made him realize that what he needed to relieve his anxiety was a woman—a real woman, not one who made her way through life on her back in some rank bawdyhouse, but a woman who was . . . what, he did not know. He had no experience with any other kind of woman, yet he felt a yearning that made him think of a home and children and a wife at his side. But he did not know how to go about it, how to find a decent woman who would take up with the likes of him.

He also had to wonder if perhaps he had not just been smitten by the sight of that particular woman, especially while he was in such a hungover condition. Almost any woman would have looked like an angel to him, he more than half suspected.

Angry after an hour of sitting there stirring up his own mental fermentations, Maxwell growled at himself and left. But in the following days he found himself back at the center of the island's life again and again. He began to feel more relaxed there, and one day took it into his head to approach a young woman—one of barely marriageable age—he had seen frequently.

She was a beautiful quadroon, with skin the color of well-cured and oiled doeskin. Though young and rather thin, she had the well-rounded buttocks of a full-grown woman. Her breasts under her gauzy, unadorned cotton blouse were small but buoyant. She carried herself with ease and a lithe grace, reminding Maxwell of a female puma.

Clydie Parkes was flattered by Maxwell's attention. After all, he was older by a few years, was a pirate, and as hard as leather. It didn't hurt that he was somewhat taller than she was and quite handsome with his dark skin, fine features, and mildly kinky hair.

Maxwell began squiring Clydie Parkes about Galveston Island, keeping her away from the rougher places, and not letting his shipmates know much—if anything—about her. He did not need to listen to their coarse commentary, nor did he have any desire to try to explain that he actually felt something for this young woman. He didn't know if any of the other pirates ever thought of settling down, but he had seen no indication of it. And he didn't want to be the first one to admit something like that out in the open.

So he and Clydie kept mostly to themselves, which was difficult considering how small the island was. But they found ways to be alone amid the crowds in the square, or walking along stretches of sandy beach away from the wharfs and the saloons and bawdyhouses.

On one of those pleasant walks, as the sun was setting behind a facade of clouds, sending shards of red striping across the beach, Clydie tugged on Maxwell's hand, pulling him into the cover of several blackjack and southern live oaks. Under the great spreading canopy of leaves, Clydie stopped and pulled Maxwell's head down to kiss her.

Maxwell obliged with an insistent willingness. Within minutes, both were naked, and Maxwell was running his determined hands and tongue along Clydie's willing body. She was inexperienced but delightfully compliant—and more than ready. She had waited a long time for this, she figured, and she planned to enjoy it.

As Clydie allowed the feel of Maxwell's battle-hardened hands to send thrills of pleasure through her, she thought of how lucky she was to have found him. It wasn't often that a girl such as she could find a man who was amenable to taking his time, and treating her like a lady. And he was so experienced, too. He would teach her the ways of lovemaking the way a real man should.

Maxwell, too, found himself enthralled as he buried himself in the curves and folds of Clydie's beautiful flesh. She was everything he could want in a woman: She had beauty, a sexual hunger to match his own, she could cook, and was well versed in other domestic chores. She was obedient without being subservient to him, and she accepted him for the man he was.

Soon such thoughts—in fact all thoughts—left them, and they surrendered to the pleasures each brought to the other. Clydie reveled in the rough-gentle touch of Maxwell's hands on her sharp-nippled breasts; Maxwell sucked in a breath of pleasure as Clydie's small hand stroked his maleness and guided him into her.

Within moments, both shuddered as a thunderstorm of ecstasy pounded through them. As small as she was, Clydie exhibited an incredible grip and tenacity as her soft womanliness clamped around his hardness. Then they lay together, arms and legs woven into a random pattern, and slept.

It was full night when they awoke, still wrapped in each other's embrace. They made love again, with as much verve and passion as they had the first time.

After Maxwell had dropped Clydie at her home and was headed back to his quarters, he thought that maybe he would put down roots. Perhaps not here, but not too far away. And definitely with Clydie Parkes. He thought the two of them could head west, deeper into Spanish territory. The Spanish and many of the Indians in the region seemed to have little problem in accepting men of different colors and races. Maxwell was certain he and Clydie would be comfortable there, and have little trouble, other than what was to be expected in such a remote place.

He planned to tell Clydie about his dream for them as soon as he saw her the next day, but when the time came, he suddenly felt shy, almost afraid. He didn't know why, but it was real to him, so he put off saying anything about it to her, instead hoping that she would see his vision just from being with him so much.

If she did, though, she gave no indication of it, and Maxwell was again considering bringing it out in the open when Lafitte called for the men to return to the ship. With precious little time before having to be aboard, Maxwell rushed to Clydie and told her.

"I don't want you to go, Jacques," she said, her voice close to a whine.

"I don' t'ink much of ze idea myself," Maxwell admitted. "But I 'ave to go. I 'ave no money for myself. If I 'ad, I would stay 'ere wit' you." When he saw her pouting, Maxwell added, "But when I come back, I will 'ave plenty of booty. Zen I will take you out into ze Spanish lands, where we will make our home, *ça va?*"

There, he thought, it was out in the open. He was pleased with the idea, and he looked happily at Clydie's face. Her expression indicated that she thought the idea was splendid. So, with a mixture of joy and sorrow, Maxwell kissed Clydie goodbye and headed toward where Lafitte's ship was tied.

As he joined his crewmates in getting the swift, deadly ship under way, Maxwell kept glancing at the shore of Galveston Island. He hoped that Clydie was there to watch him leave. He thought he saw her, and felt a lightening in his heart, and he bent back to his work with renewed verve.

He soon found that, while he missed Clydie, at times greatly, he was glad to be at sea. He relished the smell of the salt air and the raucous cries of the gulls. He felt comfortable with the soft roll of the ship under his feet, and hearing the sharp snapping of the sails. And he began to have doubts about his dream for him and Clydie. Not that he did not want to be with her. He just found it difficult to think of living on land, well away from the water, with no more chance to be aboard a ship. That was not a thought he could take lightly.

12

More ships of more countries were crisscrossing the Gulf of Mexico, which meant that Lafitte's men had a high time raiding. Their booty piled up above- and belowdecks, taken from Spanish, British, French, and American vessels. Some of it was in the form of gold, silver, and precious jewels, much more was in the more prosaic form of bales of cotton, barrels of whiskey and wine, crates of foodstuffs, and bolts of cloth. All would sell anywhere.

After only two months at sea, Lafitte ordered his ships to set sail for Galveston Island. This was a great relief to Maxwell. Lafitte could have headed for his usual base at Barataria near New Orleans, but Maxwell was counting on Lafitte's growing fondness for Galveston.

Maxwell headed for Clydie's place as soon as ship business was taken care of, which seemed to take weeks for Maxwell, though it was only days. He thought he had spotted Clydie once or twice watching the ship as he worked. But finally the last of the booty was sold and unloaded to be carted off by the buyer, and the men were free to go enjoy themselves. Maxwell raced off, coins jingling in the leather pouch he wore tied to his wide belt.

Clydie was indeed waiting for him, and was mighty happy to see him. It didn't hurt any that he had some hard coin to spend on her, which he did with abandon. Clydie, in turn, showed her gratitude in the best way she knew.

However, the young woman was not nearly so happy when it came time for Maxwell to ship out again. There was no way he could refuse, because he was almost penniless again. Clydie accepted that explanation much more easily than the other one Maxwell had tried to offer—that his pride and sense of loyalty demanded that he go. He owed everything to Lafitte and his crewmates. He could not abandon his captain now.

So he turned to reason, and showed Clydie his almost empty pockets. While Clydie Parkes was not a greedy woman, she did want her man to have some financial resources. It was the only way to start a family. So she reluctantly bid him farewell. "Godspeed, my dear Jacques," she said sadly, just after kissing him goodbye.

"Je t'aime," Maxwell responded. "But don' forget, I'll be back soon, ça va? Maybe even before you knew I am gone." He felt terrible about leaving her, but there was nothing he could do, he thought.

"That won't ever happen, dearest," Clydie said, trying unsuccessfully to smile. "I miss you already."

Maxwell nodded. There was not much he could say to that. He turned and headed for the ship, which was sitting at the wharf not far away. As the ship cast off, he once again watched Clydie diminish with distance.

Maxwell chafed at the delay. They had been away from Galveston Island for a little over a year. At first, the raiding had been very good, and they had made several trips to islands along the Gulf Coast to unload their booty, but they had not returned to Galveston. They were ashore on Barataria when Lafitte was approached by emissaries from the American government. Lafitte entertained these dignitaries in the finest fashion, providing the best wines and foods that could be procured from his own stolen stocks or from the area residents themselves.

Maxwell didn't pay much attention, though the talks lasted some days. He figured the American officials were here to try to talk the great pirate Jean Lafitte into joining their side in their war with Britain. Maxwell didn't think Lafitte could be talked into such a foolish move, so he didn't concern himself with it.

What he did think about, however, was getting off Barataria and getting back to Galveston Island, where he could be with Clydie. He thought about her a lot, and had made up his mind that this—or these, depending on how many more times Lafitte set out before returning to Galveston—would be his final voyage with Lafitte. He would take the money he got from this round of piracy, and he would use it to set up a home for himself and Clydie, and he might even try to open some kind of business, though he didn't know just what. He would worry about that later. With any luck, he would have more than enough to live on for some time while he figured out what to do next. So it came as something of a shock when he heard of Lafitte's plans.

"*Mes amis,*" Lafitte started, after gathering the men on the deck of the ship, "ze Américains, zey 'ave ask zis 'umble *homme* to come to zeir assistance. I 'ave agreed to do zis."

The pirate captain waited until the roar died down. It was clear the men were not happy, with most of their shouts having to do with the fact that they were pirates and they should not be fighting in someone else's war.

When there was mostly silence again, Lafitte shrugged. "*Mes amis,* we 'ave been together for a long time, *n'est-ce pas?* But zis t'ing I must do. Ze French, zey are 'elping ze Américains again. For zis, zey hope ze Américains will 'elp zem in ze struggle zey are facing in France. But zat is for later, *ça va?* Right now, ze fighting is 'ere, and we will be a part of it."

"What da hell fo'?" someone shouted from the gathered throng.

"If we do not fight wit' ze Américains, ze British, zey will blockade New Orleans and other ports. Zen all we will 'ave to raid out in ze ocean are British warships, *ça va?* If we 'elp ze Américains, maybe we can break ze British blockade. After ze fighting is ovair, zen we can go back to our own business."

"Why should we want to take part in this goddamn nonsense?" another crew member demanded to know.

"You men 'ave given me your word zat you will follow me. And you 'ave pledged your loyalty to me, *monsieur*. Zat is why."

"Suppose we ain't of a mind to do such a thing?" a third man shouted.

Lafitte thought about that for a few moments. "Anyone 'ere who does not wish to follow zis *homme* is free to go. But I warn you who do zat: You will nevair work with Jean Lafitte again, *monsieurs. Mais non!* And I will nevair call you *mon ami* again." He paused, leaning on the upper deck railing. "So if any of you want to go, now is ze time to do it, *monsieurs*." He straightened back up, and folded his arms across his chest.

Only two men took Lafitte up on his offer. Maxwell almost went for it, but decided at the last minute not to. Lafitte had done a lot for him, and he could not bring himself to be disloyal now. At least not here. Had they been docked at Galveston Island, Maxwell would have joined the other two in jumping ship, as it were. He would have collected his share of the money brought in by the booty, and then gone off to live his life with Clydie. But here, so far from Galveston, and with feelings of guilt roiling in his head, Maxwell decided he would have to stay put.

It was only after the battle for New Orleans itself, when he could look at things and listen to the grateful thanks of American officials in New Orleans, that Maxwell realized just how important Lafitte and his men had been in the Americans winning that battle. They had done much to prevent the British warships and supply vessels from reinforcing and resupplying the British forces on land.

Not that Maxwell cared which side really won. He had been born a slave to an American master, so he had no love for white Americans. On the other hand, he had no particular liking for the British. As far as he could tell from his contact with them, they were as reprehensible as the Americans were.

But when he heard their offer of amnesty to all of Lafitte's men, Maxwell was very glad that the Americans had won. It meant that he could not be prosecuted for any crimes he might have committed while in Lafitte's service. He proudly accepted the two pieces of paper handed to him by an American official who grinned widely, but only limply shook his hand, as if afraid to touch him.

"'Ow come I got two papers, when you and most of ze other got only one, *Monsieur le Capitaine*?" he asked Lafitte later that day.

Lafitte took the papers and looked them over. He held one up, "Zis is ze amnesty paper, *ça va?*"

Maxwell nodded.

"Zis other one, it is called a manumission paper, *mon ami*."

"And what is zat?"

"Zat means you're a free man, *mon ami. "Tu es un homme libre!"*

Maxwell was dumbstruck. He did not know what to say, nor could he have managed to say something even if he had thought of it. He simply stood, mouth agape, staring at the indecipherable words on the piece of fine paper. Finally he turned and wandered off, muttering to himself and shaking his head in amazement. This simple piece of paper changed his whole life for all time.

He was still astounded over his good fortune when he and the other men gathered in a semicircle at the fire in front of Lafitte's tent. The captain had tall mugs of wine handed out to the men, and fresh tobacco for their pipes. He pointed to several tables to his left, laden with food. "We will 'ave us one 'ell of *un féte ce soir, monsieurs*," he said with a wide grin. "But first zere is a little business zat we must get out of ze way."

Seeing that he had all the men's attention, Lafitte continued. "I 'ave been given amnesty, too. But more, I 'ave been offered a commission in *les marines des Américains*—the American Navy. But, sadly to say to zem, I turn it down. *Je suis le grand pirate Jean Lafitte*," he added proudly. "*Je ne suis pas un fantoche des Américains!*"

"So, you are going back to raiding on the seas, eh?" his first mate said more than asked.

"*Mais oui!*" Lafitte asserted. When the excited buzz from the men quieted down, the captain added, "You men, *mes amis*, are welcome to set sail wit' me again. You are loyal, true men, ones I can trust, and I would like to 'ave you all back wit' me on my ship. Are you wit' me?"

Maxwell was even more perplexed now. He wanted to get back to Clydie and begin his life with her. He had no more desire to raid merchant ships. But it would take him a month or more to get to Galveston Island if he had to do it on foot. Aboard the ship, he might be there much sooner if Lafitte decided to head there soon. It was a dilemma, and he did not like it. He kept silent as most of the other men cheered.

While the party was in full swing, Maxwell finally managed to corner Lafitte. He explained his problem to the pirate captain, ending with, "You 'ave been *très bon* to me, *Monsieur le Capitaine*, and I feel some'ow wrong in leaving you. But I 'ave Clydie waiting for me, and I want to 'ave a family."

"I understand, *monsieur*," Lafitte said. Whether he did or not, he appeared to. "I will 'ate to lose you, *mon ami*. You're a good man, Jacques, but if your life is elsewhere, I won' stop you." He paused to sip some of his wine. "But what do we do about your problem of getting back to Galveston, eh?" He thought about it some more, making Maxwell fidgety. "Well, *monsieur*, about ze best I can do is to promise you zat we will make port in Galveston as soon as is reasonable, *ça va*? Will zat do?"

"*Oui, Monsieur le Capitaine.*" Maxwell wasn't all that sure that it would be good, but he could press no more. Lafitte had made up his mind, and Maxwell would have to live with it now. He just hoped that their raids would take him closer to Galveston, so that setting into port there would make sense. And he hoped it would be soon. Then he went and joined the festivities. The more he drank, the less he worried about getting to Galveston.

It took somewhat longer than he had hoped to make his return, but not as long as he had feared. He was as anxious as a cat treading on hot stones as he worked on the ship. It had been a mighty long time since he had been back, and he wondered if Clydie would still be waiting for him. He tried to tell himself that she would be, that she loved him deeply, and would not give up on him so easily. But there was a large part of his mind that would not agree with that.

He considered jumping ship several times, but decided he could not do that to Lafitte—or to the men with whom he had worked for these past several years. So he worked and waited and fretted at the delay.

Finally, however, he was free to go ashore on his own. He bid farewell to Lafitte and to his shipmates, before heading swiftly for Clydie's. As he neared her shack, however, he slowed, and then slowed some more. He was suddenly very cautious, and began to wonder if he should even go to her house and ask about her. It had been such a long time. But he had to go through with it, and he knew it. He rapped on the door of the ramshackle house where Clydie lived with her mother and numerous siblings.

Clydie's mother came to the door. Her dark eyes registered surprise when she saw who was calling. "Clydie ain't heah," she said nervously.

"Where is she?" Maxwell asked anxiously.

"I don't know," Elvie Parkes said, more frightened than Maxwell.

"I t'ink you're not telling me ze truth, madam," Maxwell said, trying to hide his worry. "Does she live 'ere anymore?"

"No," Elvie said with a shake of the head.

"'As she gone off wit' another man?" The words

sounded foreign to him, as if someone else were speaking them.

Elvie nodded, head down. Then she looked up and stared Maxwell in the eyes. "She waited a long time fo' you, Mistah Maxwell. But we heard Mistah Lafitte joined his ship wif the Americans to fight wif them. And we thought you maybe was kilt in da fightin' since you nevah come back heah."

"Well, *madam*, as you can plainly see since I am standing 'ere in front of you, I am not kilt," Maxwell said harshly. He was growing angry now. "Where is she?"

"I ain't gonnah tell you dat, Mistah Maxwell. I sho' ain't."

"You'll tell me," Maxwell threatened, pulling his dagger. He grabbed the front of Elvie's dress and was ready to plunge the blade into her in a nonfatal spot to convince her to tell him where her daughter was. A sharp cry from a child inside the shack shook Maxwell back to his senses. He released her dress and slid the dagger away.

"*Pardonnez-moi, madam*," he said, shaken by his sudden turn to violence against an innocent person. He sighed. "Tell 'er I love 'er. *Adieu, madam*." He spun and walked off, his head high, but his heart dragging on the ground.

Unwilling to face his former shipmates, Maxwell decided he would go elsewhere, though he had no idea of where that was. He was a free man, had some money in his pouch, and had nothing to hold him anywhere. He headed northeast, following the curving Gulf of Mexico coast, retracing the path he had originally taken almost six years ago when he was still a new runaway.

Long before he reached the Mississippi River, he had decided he would follow that mighty river northward and see what the world held for him there. He had heard some stories that places up there were, if not friendly, at least not too antagonistic toward men with black skin. And he had no illusions about being treated equally, or even decently, in the slave-holding states from which he had escaped. Free man or not, he knew he would still have a hard time making a go of it.

He eventually made it to Saint Louis, where, a few months later, Giles Elgood found him toiling away as a bartender and bouncer in a foul saloon called the Hog's Breath.

Summer 1815

There was a hushed silence around the campfire along the Missouri River. A few of the men doubted the bulk of Maxwell's story, but most of them were shrewd enough to see the signs of its veracity on Maxwell's black face, and in his dark, deep-set eyes, and in the memory of that awesome scar on the former slave's shoulder that they had all seen. Even those who believed that Maxwell had exaggerated more than a little figured there were some kernels of truth in the story. Besides, none of them was about to challenge Maxwell. Not after he had handled Judd Shawcross so easily.

"You've lived a mite of a colorful life, my friend," Elgood said evenly, though one could see in his eyes that he was impressed, and perhaps a bit cowed.

"Ah, *oui*," Maxwell acknowledged. Then he laughed. "But zere are many more adventures for zis *homme* to 'ave before I am gone to 'eaven."

Elgood laughed too. "So, you're pretty certain, are you, that you're goin' to heaven?"

"*Mais oui!*" Maxwell laughed even harder. "Ze devil, he don' want no part of zis old pirate, *n'est-ce pas?*"

"I reckon he wouldn't. You'd probably scare that evil son of a bitch half to death."

"I would try, *mais oui.*" He let out an exaggerated sigh. "But I t'ink zat fellow 'as got 'imself zat way already, *ça va?*"

The men spent the remainder of the day resting, letting their muscles recover somewhat from the rigors of the journey. They snoozed or gambled a little. One or two were seen reading—to themselves, unless some of those who could not read asked them to do so aloud. They repaired equipment or cleaned weapons and utensils. Few did anything very strenuous; their regular work was plenty taxing enough, and they could see no reason to abuse their bodies even more with too much physical activity.

The next morning, however, they were back at their posts on the boat, the boatmen cordelling, rowing, or poling the keelboat up the powerful river. The hunters were ashore, while other trappers rested on the top of the keelboat's cabin, keeping watch for any trouble. For days at a time the traveling was quiet, but then it would be punctuated by violence or humor or danger. At times, it was all three.

The journey upriver led to several more encounters with Indians—some friendly and some not. The trappers managed to come out of them with no loss of life. There were a few wounds now and then, and some trade goods passed around to ensure safe passage when the Indians would allow it.

Each confrontation, however, even the peaceful ones, prepared the men a little more. As each band or tribe was encountered, the few old hands would hastily try to explain a little about their customs and language and ways. The men picked up on it fairly quickly, and with each new run-in, peaceful or otherwise, they became a little more confident in themselves and in their companions.

But the tribes were only a small part of their problems. When on shore, the men had to worry about facing grizzly bears and wolves, both of which seemed to roam in unlimited numbers. Two men died at the fangs and claws of grizzlies, making the others highly touchy about running into them. It got to the point where the hunters would shoot a grizzly whenever one was found within rifle range. Sometimes they would take the hide and claws and teeth to use themselves or for trade with the Indians. At other times the men just let the carcass lie there and rot. Few of them had much use for bear meat, and while the rendered fat was highly useful, there was no dearth of the animals, so they were never low on it.

Even more awe-inspiring were those rare occasions when an old buffalo bull, crotchety with the infirmities of an old age it could not understand, would charge a group of hunters. The men usually had little trouble in dropping the bull in his tracks, but the first few times it happened, several of the men were so struck by the sight that they froze, and were saved only when those with cooler heads took control and ended the peril.

The river itself posed its own problems above and beyond the sheer mind-numbing, exhausting strenuousness of propelling the vessel up it. The many rapids took a heavy toll on the men's strength. It was hellacious trying to control the suddenly fragile-seeming keelboat through the pounding, rushing, frothy water, trying to steer the bouncing, jerking craft around the boulders and over the sunken rocks that were churning the water into such a wild boil.

Even worse were the waterfalls. The travelers encountered a number of them, including several huge ones. When faced with such a formidable obstacle, the keelboat would be brought up onto shore where everything was unloaded. Then, while some of the men cut logs, the rest of the crew carried the pirogues—big dugout canoes—and everything from the keelboat overland to the other side of the falls.

Once that was done came the monumental task of hauling the keelboat itself around the falls. The logs that had been cut earlier were employed as rollers. Then, using brute strength, the men dragged the fragile wooden ship across the rollers inch by painful, muscle-draining, gut-wrenching inch.

On the other side of the roaring falls, the keelboat was inspected to make sure it would still float, then was relaunched. Everything was loaded back on board, the pirogues were filled, and they departed again.

A good many of the younger men, on this trek for the first time, took to complaining regularly, even though the bulk of the hardest work fell to the boatmen. The traders were pressed into service far more frequently than they wanted, and carped about it incessantly. Elgood tried to calm the men down regularly, but it seemed to have little effect. The venture's captain, however, noticed that the men assigned to Maxwell did very little complaining. He wondered why, so one evening he strolled over to where Maxwell and his small crew had their fire. He sat, took the proffered cup of coffee, and then asked straight out how Maxwell was keeping his men quiet.

Maxwell grinned a little, and ran a forefinger across his slim mustache. "You boys want to tell *Monsieur le Capitaine* 'ow I do it?"

"I'll tell him," Beecher piped up, almost eagerly. "You see, Cap'n," he said, "Mister Maxwell over there has hisself a right good way with words, I'm tellin' ya. After we'd been harpin' on all our difficulties for a lot longer'n he really wanted to hear it, he jist set us all down at the fire like this here one night and he tol' us, '*Mes amis*, zis complaining is gotting on my nerves. *Mais oui!* And I won' put up wit' it much longer, *ça va?* If you don' like ze situation, go back, or stay where you are. I don' care. I jus' want you all to *fermez tes bouches*— shut your mouths. If you don' do zat for *moi*, I will see zat one day you are left behind out here to make your own way wherever you want at your own pace, *n'est-ce pas?*' We been obedient fellers ary since."

Everyone—including Maxwell—laughed at Beecher's uncanny imitation of Maxwell's speech.

"So you just threatened to leave 'em behind, eh, Jacques?" Elgood asked. "And that worked?"

"*Oui et oui*. You don' hear *mes amis* complaining, did you?" Maxwell answered, as if it was all so simple that it didn't need explanation.

"Well, no, I ain't heard 'em complainin', which is why I come over here in the first place—to find out what you've done," Elgood said with a nod. "Reckon I'll have to try that on the others." He started to get up, but Maxwell tugged him back down.

"You better t'ink zis t'ing t'rough, *Monsieur le Capitaine*."

"Why's that, Jacques?" Elgood was puzzled.

"Zat won' work wit' everyone, *monsieur*. Unless you do it right," Maxwell said.

"What's that mean?" Elgood questioned, annoyed because he thought he was being toyed with. He considered himself both intelligent and perceptive, and it worried him just a little that this unlettered former slave might have been able to figure out something that he could not.

"Ze men 'ave to know you will done what you say you will done," Maxwell explained. "If zey t'ink you don't have *des couilles*—the balls—to done what you said you will done, ze men, zey won' listen to you about zis, and maybe not anyt'ing else either."

Elgood nodded. That made sense. He wished he had thought of it himself. "So you boys knew Jacques'd make good on his threat?" he asked.

The others nodded.

"We've worked with him long enough now," Thornton said, "that we know he'll do whatever he says. Good or bad. 'Course, it took Pete over there a lesson before he knew for certain. Ain't that right, you dopey bastard?" Thornton asked, looking at a tall, big, slope-shouldered fellow with a round, pasty face.

Pete Lepari was usually a cheerful man, and he grinned a little now. "Took a time, yeah," he said with a nod, then he went back to gnawing on his fingernails. He did it so often that he usually had them down to the quick, and they occasionally bled a little.

Elgood sat there, sipping from the coffee mug, thinking it over. He was not sure at all that the men would believe he would leave someone behind. They generally did obey his commands, but he now suspected that was solely because he was the commander of this expedition. He could not recall any of the men—except perhaps Maxwell—obeying him out of respect.

"I don't mean to overstep my bounds, *Monsieur le Capitaine*," Maxwell said quietly, "but you 'ave a problem, and zere is only one way, maybe, to fix it."

"Explain, Jacques, if you would."

"Tell ze men zat if zey do not contain zeir griping, you will leave ze loudest troublemaker behind to fend for himself."

"That's no problem," Elgood said. "But how do I get 'em to believe I would leave one of 'em behind?"

"Because you will *leave* one of zem behind," Maxwell said simply. "Ze first time ze men zey violate your rule, you pick ze one wit' ze most or ze loudest complaints, you strip 'im of 'is weapons and everyt'ing else ze company provided for 'im, give 'im a knife, maybe, and a couple days' supply of meat. Zen turn 'im loose."

"I can guarantee you, Cap'n," Beecher put in, "that you won't have no more trouble from the others."

Elgood nodded, picking the plan over in his head. Finally he said, "That's all well and good, my friends, but there are problems in that, too. For one, I'd not want the death of a man on my head."

Maxwell shrugged. Life was too ephemeral, and could be snuffed out incredibly swiftly, no matter how much one tried to prevent that. Worrying about someone who through his own troublemaking brought on his own demise was useless as far as Maxwell was concerned.

"There's another reason, though, and a damn more pragmatic one at that."

"Which is?" Thornton asked for his mentor.

"We need all the men we have. We've already lost a couple. We can't afford to lose many more without jeopardizin' the entire expedition. I especially can't just turn one out for complainin' too much."

Maxwell had not thought of that. "Zen t'ink of some other punishment, *Monsieur le Capitaine*," he suggested. "You must do somet'ing to one of zem. Somet'ing zat will let zem know wit'out question zat you are to be obeyed. It will do your command good, bot' now in zis case, and in ze future, when someone t'inks to cause trouble for you."

"That I can do, my friend," Elgood said, standing. "Thank you, Jacques, you've been a big help."

"*De rien, Monsieur le Capitaine.*" He was interested to see what Elgood would do about all this.

He found out the next morning when Elgood called his men into a group and addressed them. "We've come a long way, men," he started. "But we got a heap of miles yet to cover. And it don't make the goin' any easier when the majority of you are complainin' regularly. So I'm tellin' you boys right here and now to put a stop to this endless carpin'. There'll be hell to pay if you don't."

"Like what?" one of the men asked.

"Disobey me, boy, and you'll find that justice will be swift and certain," Elgood said evenly. Now that he had made up his mind, he was strong and sure in his purpose. He would not falter.

"Sounds like a heap of hogwash to me," one of the men said with a snort. "You can't stop the men from gripin' now and again."

"That's a fact, boy," Elgood responded, not sure who had made the statement. "And I'm not tryin' to do that. Hell, everybody's got a right to complain now and then. A man wouldn't be a man if he couldn't do that. But I'm not talkin' about such a thing. What I'm talkin' about is the incessant protestin' and whinin' about the food and the work and every other damn thing that can be thought of. The work is hard. Damn hard. No one here's denyin' that, but you should've known that right from the start.

"As for the food, hell, it's a damn sight better than most of you ever got back in the Settlements. There's more than a few of you boys who've plumped up like a hog for market since we set off."

The traveling was relatively quiet for a couple of days, as the men assessed Elgood's determination to reduce the number and vociferousness of their complaints. Then a man named Tom Corcoran decided to challenge the captain. He had a low opinion of Elgood anyway, and he figured this was the time to show the commander that he really didn't have much control over his men. His complaints began loud and grew in intensity and frequency throughout the day. As the day wore on, the other men began to wonder if Elgood was indeed going to do anything. Some joined in, starting slowly but picking up steam as the hours passed.

Corcoran thought he was going to get away with all his complaining, and he was elated. He figured he would do damn near anything he wanted now, and no one would bother him. So it was a great surprise to him, when Elgood gathered the men together, that he was called to the front.

"You remember what I told you and the others just a couple of days ago, Corcoran?" Elgood asked.

"I reckon. So?"

"You broke the rules, boy, and now you'll pay the price for it."

"What're you gonna do to me, you son of a bitch?" Corcoran asked warily, growing defensive.

Elgood ignored him. He turned to Maxwell and nodded.

Maxwell strode up to Corcoran. "'And over your guns and your shooting possibles," he ordered.

"Like hell I will," Corcoran snapped. He glanced at Elgood and then back to Maxwell. But he spoke to Elgood. "Tell this black bastard to git away from me before I smite him down, Cap'n," he said harshly.

The next thing he knew, he was on his back in the dirt with Maxwell's right boot on his chest, holding him down. Blood flowed from his nose and the corner of a lip.

"Your guns, *monsieur*," Maxwell said evenly.

14

"You better do as he says, Corcoran," Elgood said calmly.

"I can't do that whilst he's standin' on my chest, Cap'n," Corcoran snapped.

Maxwell moved his foot and stepped back a little. "Don' try not'ing else, *monsieur*, or ze next time I will 'urt you instead of jus' knock you down."

Corcoran nodded, and rose slowly. He eased out his pistol and handed it butt first to Maxwell, who in turn tossed it to Thornton. Next came the rifle, which Maxwell handed behind him without looking, until Beecher took it. The shooting bag and powder horns came next and were taken by Lepari.

"Turn around, *monsieur*," Maxwell said. When a suddenly very nervous Corcoran did so, Maxwell stepped up, knife in hand, and slit Corcoran's shirt down the back. He jammed the knife between his teeth—a not unfamiliar place for it—and then ripped the shirt until it was hanging by shreds down Corcoran's legs.

"Hey, what the hell're you doin', you . . ."

Corcoran started, until Maxwell cuffed him across the ear.

"*Fermez la bouche,*" Maxwell snapped. "And keep it shut." He spun Corcoran until the trapper was facing Elgood, who was still standing on a large rock.

"You're a damn fool, Corcoran," Elgood said roughly. "And now you'll pay for your defiance. Your insubordination is worth fifteen lashes. You have anythin' to say before we commence?"

Corcoran's eyes were huge with fear, anger, and surprise. "That ain't right, Cap'n," he stammered. "That's too . . . "

"If all you're gonna do is whine some more, boy, you can put a halt to it right now. There's not a man here who's got the time or inclination to listen to your babble. You have somethin' of merit to say, proceed. If you don't, shut the hell up and take your punishment like a man."

Corcoran had a sinking feeling in his stomach. He had always known his smart mouth was going to get him in trouble, but he had always let it rule him, as it had today. He tried to work up anger against Elgood, or any of the other men, but he found he could not do it. His conscience would not let him shift the blame for this on to anyone else. It was his own doing, and he had to face up to the punishment. He just hoped he could live through the harsh whipping.

Corcoran was soon tied to a tree, his feet together, his arms spread wide to the side. His bare, pale white back gleamed in the tree-dappled afternoon sunlight on the riverbank.

"Commence," Elgood said. He got no enjoyment out of such things, but it was necessary, and he had no compunction about carrying through on it. The success of their mission relied on strong discipline, and he could not let anyone get away with such insubordination as Corcoran had shown.

Elgood had gone to Maxwell sometime during the day and sought his help. Maxwell was one of the few men Elgood thought he could put his absolute trust in now.

"Sure I will 'elp you, *Monsieur le Capitaine*," Maxwell said. "What do you want me to did?"

"Disarm him, tie him to a tree, and administer the lashes," Elgood said. He figured that since Maxwell had faced the whip himself, both as a slave and while aboard Lafitte's ship, he would be happy to be on the administering end of it for a change.

"I will disarm 'im, *oui*," Maxwell said reflectively. "And I will cut 'is shirt from 'im, and tie 'im to a tree. But I will not do ze whipping. *Mais non!*" He was angry now, and perhaps a little fear showed in his eyes.

"Why not?" Elgood asked, shocked.

"I don' 'ave to give you a reason, *Monsieur le Capitaine*," Maxwell said. "If you t'ink zat is insubordination, zen you will 'ave to whip me *aussi*. But I tell you now, *monsieur*, I won' done zis."

Elgood looked with surprise at the former slave. He wondered how he could have been so wrong in his thinking. Just looking at Maxwell, he could tell that nothing in heaven or hell could sway the black to change his mind. He could not understand it, but he was fairly sure he didn't want to understand it.

"I will fought 'im, if you ask me zat. I will kill 'im. I will cut out 'is 'eart and eat it in front of you, if you wanted such a t'ing. But I will not whip another man. Not for you, *Monsieur le Capitaine*. Not for anybody."

Elgood nodded, taken aback by Maxwell's vehemence, but accepting it too. "I'm sorry, Jacques," he said quietly. "I thought you would appreciate such a . . . " He paused, cleared his throat, and said, "Well, then, if you would just disarm him and make him ready, I'll have someone else apply the lash. That acceptable to you?"

"*Oui.*"

So now he stood, eyes blank, arms across his chest as Corcoran's brigade leader—John Peabody—flexed his arms and shook out the short cat-o-nine-tails.

"Proceed," Elgood ordered.

Peabody snapped his arm forward and the leather ends of the whip tore across Corcoran's naked back, eliciting a startled hiss of pain.

Maxwell lasted for three lashes before he pushed his way through the gathering of men and moved off to his camp. Even there he could hear the whip, and Corcoran's howls of pain. He finally went down to the river and squatted on a small pebbly patch. With trees around, and the rush of the river over some rocks nearby, he could almost pretend that he could not hear anything. He spit into an eddy, angry at himself for being this way; angry at Corcoran for having been stupid enough to challenge Elgood's authority.

When he figured the whipping was over,

Maxwell stood and moved back toward camp. Some men were just cutting Corcoran down from the tree.

"A couple of you boys take him into the cabin on the keelboat and tend to him," Elgood ordered. "But be quick about it. There's a heap of work left to be done here before the night arrives, and we'll need all hands. Just leave him down there when you're done with him and git your ornery hides back to work."

"Where you been, Jacques?" Thornton asked as he and Beecher stopped next to Maxwell.

"Here and about, *mes amis*," Maxwell answered quietly.

"Didn't you stay and watch?" Beecher asked. He was the cockier of the two, and more prone to speak without thinking.

"Why would I done zat?" Maxwell asked, glaring at Beecher.

The young man was not too put off. "Well, it sure taught ol' Tom a lesson, I suspect," he said almost gleefully. "Damn, though, that must've hurt like the dickens."

"I can arrange it so zat you know for sure, *mon ami*," Maxwell said coldly.

"Ah, come on, Jacques," Beecher started, but he clamped his mouth shut when he saw the look on Maxwell's dark face. He might have been headstrong and rash, but he wasn't insane.

"Let me tell you somet'ing, *mon ami*," Maxwell said harshly. "Zere is not'ing good about a flogging. I can tell you zis from my experience, Lucius. You would not be making so light of zis if you 'ad ever felt ze lash on your back. Believe me when I say zis to you."

"I didn't mean nothin' by it, Jacques," Beecher said, trying to smooth things over. "It's jist that I never saw anything like that and all and . . . " His voice fell off as he realized how dumb he was beginning to sound.

"All I ask, *mon ami*, is zat you stop to t'ink about t'ings before you made light of zem, *ça va?*

"I understand, Jacques," Beecher said, chastened. He hurried off with Thornton, glad to be away from the hard stare of the former slave.

It was fall by the time the expedition reached the confluence of the Yellowstone and Missouri Rivers. From there, they took the Yellowstone southwest to where it joined the Tongue River. As soon as they arrived there, Elgood put the men to work. Some spread out into surrounding areas to cut logs, others started trapping, since everyone who was hired as a trapper now knew his business. Many of the trappers also hunted. Other men pulled rocks up from either of the rivers, to be used for fireplaces.

When enough logs were available to get started, the men began building the small "fort" in which the captain and the boatmen would stay the winter. The trappers would be spending the cold months with some of the friendly Indian tribes, trading, trapping when possible, and building up good relations for the future so the company could continue to turn a nice profit.

The men worked fast on constructing the fort in the V-shaped patch of land between the two rivers. It was on a slight rise, which Elgood hoped would keep them from getting flooded out, though that was a worry that would not have to be considered until spring.

While they worked, a band of Crows showed up and asked to trade. Elgood nodded, and allowed five of the warriors inside the log stockade of the fort-in-progress.

Maxwell sat close to Elgood, but almost opposite him. He wanted to watch the captain conduct business, thinking he might learn some things. He was right. This was where Elgood shone, Maxwell found out. Though the entire parley was carried on in sign language, Elgood drove a hard bargain, and came out well ahead when it was all said and done. Among the things Elgood ended up with were two dozen Crow ponies.

When the Crows had moved on, Maxwell went to Elgood, who was sitting out on the flat away from the fort. He leaned his back against a rotting log, legs stretched out in front of him. He was writing in his ledger, using a quill pen and a small bottle of ink. He put the book and quill aside when Maxwell strolled up.

"What can I do for you, Jacques?" Elgood asked. He was feeling considerably better these days. They had made it here mostly intact, and had lost none of the trade goods. He had already had one successful trade with the Crows. The fort was progressing well, and even the weather was cooperating.

"Mind if I sit here a bit, *Monsieur le Capitaine*?" Maxwell countered.

"Of course not, Jacques."

Maxwell squatted rather than sat, pulled out a

pipe, filled it and lit it. Elgood followed suit. They smoked for a while in silence. Finally Maxwell said, "I was impressed wit' you, *Monsieur le Capitaine*, in your trading wit' ze Crows."

"Thank you, Jacques. I certainly think I got the better of those boys this time."

"Are ze Crows trustworthy Innians, *Capitaine*?"

Elgood shrugged, but sat puffing his pipe. At last he said, "I reckon they're about as trustworthy a group of Indians as you're going to find out in these parts, Jacques."

"Which is to say not at all, eh?" Maxwell asked perceptively.

"You catch on fast, my friend," Elgood responded with a slight grin. He sighed. "The Crows've been friendly with Lisa's brigades since way the hell back in Oh-Seven when a feller named Colter come out here and traveled amongst them. The way I heard it, Colter fought alongside the Crows against some Blackfeet—now those are some mean Indians, boy—and handled himself well. Seems the Crows took to him after that, and so have shown considerable courtesy toward company men."

"Zat is good, *n'est-ce pas*?" Maxwell asked. "But you don' sound like you t'ink zat."

"I been out here four times now, Jacques, and I can plainly say I still don't know what to make of the damned Crows. They've never done anything against the company or its employees. At least that I'm aware of. They trade with us regularly and have been hospitable, but I just don't trust 'em. And it's not just because they're red men. I don't know."

Elgood ground to a halt and puffed harshly at his pipe for a bit, sending up roiling little puffs of poisonous smoke that circled his head like his own little storm cloud.

"They're a strange and mysterious people, Jacques," Elgood finally said. "Handsome, of course, as you no doubt saw."

Maxwell nodded. He had, indeed, taken note of the attractiveness of a couple of the young women who had been with the band.

"Excellent horsemen, too. Best I ever saw. I've never seen 'em in battle, but I've heard they are superb warriors. They're a clean and industrious people, but there's somethin' about the way they carry themselves that makes me distrust them. It's arrogance, I think. They're a damn prideful people, and it shows in everything they do, to the extent where sometimes it seems they're almost contemptuous of us."

Maxwell smiled just a little around the stem of his pipe. "Zey probably 'ave reason for zat, *Capitaine*."

"Maybe they do, Jacques, but it makes me damn uneasy around them. I always have the feelin' that they're just waitin' for us to let our guards down a little and then they'll strike." He sighed again. "It's probably just me conjurin' up demons where there aren't any."

"*Peut-etré, Capitaine.* Perhaps." Maxwell pushed his broad-brimmed felt hat back on his head a little.

"Regardless, Jacques, promise me that you'll be wary around those Indians," Elgood said.

"*Bien sûr.* Certainly. I 'ave no desire to 'ave my

'air end up on ze lodgepole of some Crow chief, *Capitaine. Mais non.* Zat would not suit me at all. If zey even do zat." He was not sure. Those with experience had explained some of the folkways of many of the tribes, and scalping and hanging the resultant trophy on a tipi lodgepole seemed to be one of the most common practices. Still, he was not sure those men had not been fooling him, trying to scare him and the others.

"Oh, they do that, all right, Jacques," Elgood said. "A contemptible habit. One of many such unsavory customs kept by those savages and others."

"Every people has zeir own ways, *Monsieur le Capitaine,*" Maxwell said with a shrug. "I would wager zat zere are many of your customs—or mine—zat would offend zese Innians."

"I suppose you're right on that, Jacques." He paused. "What the men taught you about these Indians on the way out was pretty much all true," Elgood continued. "They might've embellished things a little in the tellin', but basically it was all the truth. The Indians out here have ways that are very strange to us, and they're adamant that some of them be observed. It can lead to trouble. Bear that in mind when you venture out this winter."

Maxwell nodded, and stood. "I will, *Monsieur le Capitaine.* Now, you 'ave work, and so do I."

More Crows came to trade over the next few weeks, and Elgood managed to barter for a few horses from each band that visited. By the time the fort was built, the expedition had enough horses for all the men who would be heading out for the winter.

Just over a month after arriving at the confluence of the Tongue and Yellowstone Rivers, the small brigades began riding out.

Using a map drawn up for him by one of the men who had been out here before, Maxwell and his small crew, including his two friends Henry Thornton and Lucius Beecher, rode out, crossing the Yellowstone and heading southwest along the Tongue, toward the heart of Absaroka, the Crows' highly desirable homeland. Though none tried to show it, all the men were nervous.

15

The men rode toward the Bighorn Mountains, which they could dimly see on the horizon. All of them were awed at the incredible vastness of the country. It was a trackless prairie that ran on infinitely, a land covered with browning grass that went from ridge to ridge, forever.

The landscape teemed with wildlife—grizzly bears; swift pronghorn antelope; large elk, the bulls bugling as they vied for the attention of the does; deer; rabbits; curious prairie dogs by the millions; huge herds of buffalo with their new coats of thick winter hair; rattlesnakes, found in hissing jumbled piles under sagebrush or sunning themselves out in the open; coyotes; wolves running in packs, their eyes stark and vicious.

Only Maxwell had encountered anything like this before, and that was the Gulf of Mexico, that endless expanse of water. But this was somehow different, somehow more nerve-racking than the sea. At sea, he had the ship around him, and thus some control, or so he could tell himself, unless a storm came. But out here, the dangers were so many, and there was no haven, no large, well-made ship with strong sails, a powerful keel, knowledgeable crew.

No, out here on the land—the open land—the weather could arise as swiftly and as dangerously as at sea. On ship you had a good chance of riding it out, but where could one ride out a storm here? There was no place to hide. The gullies could fill with rushing water in moments, sweeping away men and animals almost as an afterthought. Rivers, too, could become turbulent torrents in the blink of an eye. The tops of ridges might offer some safety, but a man couldn't always get to one, and even if he did, there was the lightning, which tended to strike at men who sat on exposed ridges.

There were the animals to contend with. Poisonous, touchy rattlesnakes did not like being disturbed. Testy elk and buffalo bulls, their blood running high in the rutting season, were unpredictable, prone to charging when the riders entered their territory.

Just the massive size of some of the buffalo herds caused problems, as the men would have to ride through them sometimes for two or three days at a time, unable to catch more than a catnap in the saddle. One slip and they would be lost forever, trampled into the dust by millions of hooves.

And the men had long ago learned that they could never predict what a grizzly would do at any time. The trappers, especially the highly superstitious Jacques Maxwell, began to believe that the huge hump-necked bears were evil, and that their attacks were concerted and planned.

Worse than the danger of any of the animals was the possibility of trouble with Indians. The trading party was traversing a land that many tribes rode over, hunted on, and fought in. In their first two weeks of traveling after leaving the fort, Maxwell's small band had come across Indians five times. Four encounters had been peaceful, and the bands of different people had gone their own ways after an exchange of gifts—weighted more heavily with the whites giving—and everyone pleased.

But one band of Sioux proved to be more recalcitrant. Led by a bellicose young warrior, the Sioux demanded more gifts than the whites had proffered.

"You must show your respect for the great Lakota warrior Tall Elk," the belligerent young man said arrogantly, using signs to communicate.

"If Tall Elk is such a great warrior," Maxwell signed calmly, "then he has little need for the poor goods I could give him."

Tall Elk nodded, but said with his hands, "I will take your rifle. That is a fitting gift." He held out his hand.

Using sign language as best he could, Maxwell calmly tried to assuage Tall Elk without giving the Lakota what he wanted. He had little success, and Tall Elk began to grow angry. His hand signals were clipped, signifying his irritation.

Finally Maxwell had his fill of this supercilious young warrior. Over his shoulder, he said, "Better got ready, *mes amis*. Zere will be trouble, I t'ink. And soon." He signed to Tall Elk that the parley was over and that the small presents he had spread out for the war leader and his three men were no longer being offered.

Tall Elk's eyes bulged, and a vein throbbed strongly in his forehead. "You will die now, white-eyes," he said in signs. "All of you." He turned and spit out a string of Lakota.

As his three warriors rose, reaching for their weapons, Maxwell said quietly, "Now, *mes amis*."

Several pistols rang out, and three Lakotas fell to the ground, dead or dying.

Tall Elk jumped to his feet, furious, and a little frightened. He wrenched out his war club—a buffalo horn filled with sand to give it weight and heft, and then sealed with wood. It was attached to a stout wood handle. On his left forearm was a shield. He began chanting.

It sent an eerie shudder slithering up Maxwell's spine. He wasn't sure what it meant, until he remembered something one of the experienced hands had told him.

"What the hell's he wailin' about?" Beecher asked, holding his hands over his ears.

"I t'ink it's 'is deat' song. You remember what John Peabody said one time? Some of zese Innians, zey sing a song to make zemselves ready to die. I t'ink zat's what zis one is doing."

"Sounds like a damn fool notion to me," Beecher offered tightly.

Maxwell shrugged. He disagreed, but he could not let his superstitions keep him from doing what needed to be done. "If you attack me, you'll die," Maxwell said to Tall Elk in signs.

Despite the war club and shield, Tall Elk was able to sign that he was ready to die, and would prefer it.

"Take your men and bring them back to your people," Maxwell signed. "They should be buried properly."

"I can't," Tall Elk said in signs. "I can't face my people after having let them be killed."

"Yes, you can," Maxwell responded in kind. "You and your few men couldn't stand up against our guns. You were outnumbered and we were better armed. There's no shame in that."

Tall Elk looked skeptical, but seemed to be considering the idea. Suddenly his chanting ended, and he slid his war club away. As Tall Elk bent and lifted one of his friends, Maxwell stepped up to him and signed, "We'll help you."

The Lakota looked hatefully at Maxwell for a moment, but then nodded once, curtly.

"Henri, you and Pierre and George help zis warrior. You others keep watch in case zere are more of zem around."

It took only a few minutes to load the bodies on the warriors' own ponies and send them on their way. Maxwell stood, watching as the proud Tall Elk rode off, back straight, his quiver swaying with his horse's movement.

"What're you thinkin', Jacques?" Thornton asked, stopping alongside of him.

"I'm t'inking zat ze world is a strange place, *mon ami.* Zat Tall Elk, 'e could 'ave been a good warrior, I t'ink. But 'e let 'is pride get in 'is way. And because of zat, t'ree of 'is men is killed." He shook his head. "Damn foolish. Damn foolish," he muttered.

"You all right?" Thornton asked. He was a little worried. Maxwell had never been quite this melancholy before, and Thornton didn't like it.

There was silence for some moments, before Maxwell shook the gloom off him, doing so almost literally. He smiled at his young companion. *"Bien sûr, mon ami.* But of course. Now, let's go. *Vite.* Zere is much traveling to be done yet."

More annoying than the dangers, which were expected and thus somewhat planned for, were the little things. Like the wind. The group had noticed it the day they had left Elgood's winter fort, and they wondered why they had never taken note of it before then. It blew incessantly, a steady, frustrating, vexatious drone that never ceased. It would get worse at times, of course, when a storm would brew up and push down over them. But even on the finest of days, which were few and far between at this time of year, the wind sighed across the prairies, wrapping around the men's ears and crawling inside, there to hum and pulsate until the trappers thought they would go mad.

Considering that it was almost October, the wind was usually cold, too, bringing an ominous hint of the winter to come. Their water supplies had a touch of ice on them many mornings, and the sun seemed to throw a lot less warmth than it had done just a couple of weeks before. They also ran into snow and sleet at times.

"Zis *homme,* 'e don' like zis cold and ze snow," Maxwell said one night as he and his small band sat around a buffalo-chip fire. Snow flurries were falling, but were being whipped into a frenzy by the blustery wind. It was an entirely unpleasant day.

"Well, best get used to it, you gripin' ol' fart," Beecher said. "It's gonna get a heap worse."

Maxwell shook his head. He had never run into such weather, having spent his whole life until now in a warm climate. He could predict, however, that what they had already seen, weather-wise, boded ill for the future. He shuddered a little, thinking he could feel winter's frigid hand tighten on his chest a little. He did not like it.

After roughly a month of travel, they came upon a band of Crows somewhere in the Bighorn Mountains. Maxwell stopped his men on a shelf of rock halfway up a mountain a mile from the Indian camp. He sat there a bit, wondering whether he should make the last part of the ride down there. It was what he and his little brigade were here for, but he was reluctant to do it.

Finally he shrugged. "You men ready?" he asked. When he got a gaggle of nervous nods, he let his horse start picking its way down the mountainside. Maxwell was still quite uncomfortable on the back of a horse. He had only rarely been on a horse before he had left the fort, and those times had been mostly short jaunts. Now, after almost a month of being constantly in the hastily made, primitive saddle, he was sore and irritable.

Facing the thought of riding down the side of a mountain did nothing to improve his humor. He had little faith in the animal's ability to safely carry him to the large meadow below, especially when the rocks were covered with a light dusting of new snow.

He made it unscathed, though, and thanked Dangbe, the supreme voodoo deity. The men rode forward, moving slowly through the soft sifting of feathery snow. Maxwell rode in the lead, his men spread out in a ragged vee behind him, the pack animals in the center, protected.

Before they were halfway across the meadow, they spotted a group of Crow warriors galloping toward them. Moments later, Maxwell had his men halt and wait. He touched the small magic ouanga bag that hung around his neck under his shirt. He thought he would need the luck and the protection it brought. Before long, they were surrounded. The Crow warriors looked competent and tough, though by no means hostile.

"What are you doing in the land of the Absaroka?" one man asked, speaking in Crow and also signing.

"My friends and I have come here to trade with the Crows," Maxwell signed back. "We come from the great Missouri Fur Company, whose chief, Manuel Lisa, you should know."

The warrior nodded. "We know of this chief." He paused. "I am Blue Smoke," he said in signs. "We will welcome the men of the Trading Chief into our village. Come, we will have a feast in your honor, and then we will trade."

Maxwell's head bobbed in acceptance. He and his men followed the Crows toward the village, observing their hosts as they rode.

The Crows were tall, fine-featured men who

sat their ponies as if they had been born on them. They rode proudly, even arrogantly, seemingly confident that no other horsemen were their equals. The parts of the Crows' buckskin clothing that the visitors could see were beaded and adorned with dyed porcupine quills. The workmanship on the decorations was excellent. Some were clad in coats made of thick wool blankets; others were wrapped in buffalo robes or bear hides. Each had a quiver of arrows with an unstrung bow slung across his back. Two had lances. Blue Smoke carried an old trade musket. Each man's hair was long, with one warrior's hanging down his back outside his blanket coat until it flowed onto his pony's rump. Maxwell had never seen the like.

The camp itself was more orderly than Maxwell would have expected. He had thought he would see a rank village of ragged tipis and indolent people. What he found was a comfortable-looking place, with well-tended, brightly painted lodges. Smoke drifted from the tops of the tipis to mingle with the light snowfall and the grayness of the day. Outside each lodge there was a tripod, which Maxwell learned upon closer examination held the weapons of the man who lived there—lances, bow and arrows, shield, tomahawk, war club.

Children ran around, clad as their parents were in buckskins and blanket coats. They played and hollered as children everywhere did, though at the approach of the visitors, most of the littler children stopped and stared, partly in awe, partly in fear, but with interest. Women toted firewood from where trees grew along the river, or skimmed buckets of water from the river itself.

Dogs snapped and snarled—at the visitors and at each other, until someone would throw something at them to scatter them momentarily.

One thing that Maxwell noticed was the lack of horses. He had been told by the trappers on the keelboat that the Crows had more horses than any other tribe; that each band had ponies numbering into the hundreds. But there were very few horses here in the camp, or anywhere within seeing distance. Maxwell wondered if this band was particularly destitute of horseflesh or if the animals were kept elsewhere.

They finally stopped outside a large lodge that was decorated with many scenes. Maxwell assumed that the occupant must be a great chief, for he had heard on the journey upriver that such paintings were a record of the occupant's deeds.

A tall, broad-shouldered Crow stood outside the lodge. His hair was very long, reaching almost to his knees. The black mane was highlighted with streaks of gray, though his face was mostly unlined yet. He held a thick blanket around him at chest level, leaving his buckskin-clad shoulders out in the weather. When the group stopped in front of him, the man handed the blanket to a plump young woman. "I am Great Bear of the Absaroka," he said with signs—and verbally, his great voice suited to a man of his stature. "I welcome the friends of the Trading Chief to our village."

"You know why we are here?" Maxwell signed, his face showing surprise.

Great Bear nodded

"We are glad to be in Great Bear's village," Maxwell said, shaking off the surprise a little. "And we have gifts for the great chief of the Absaroka." He had learned his lessons well from Giles Elgood and the other experienced hands.

16

Maxwell's small band—Henry Thornton, Lucius Beecher, Pete Lepari, Nils Nordgren, Milt Richwine, and George Stroud—enjoyed the festivities, though all remained cautious, mostly out of fear. They could not quite believe they were sitting in a Crow village along Wolf Creek in the foothills of the Bighorn Mountains, watching the Indians dance, feasting on rare and unusual foods—some of which they would have second thoughts about once they learned what they were—and feeling almost as if they belonged here.

As the evening progressed, Beecher, always the impetuous one, leaned over and asked Maxwell, "You think these boys'd take any exception to it if I was to take one of these squaws off into the bushes?"

"For carnal purposes, I suppose?" Maxwell responded with a grin.

"Hell, why else?"

"I don' 'ave ze slightest notion what zese Innians t'ink about anyt'ing, *mon ami*. Considerin' 'ow savage zey can be, I'd use some caution."

"But this one squaw's hangin' all over me, Jacques," Beecher said almost plaintively. "I ain't got all that much experience in these matters, ya understand, but I can't help but think this here one has got the urge to have this ol' boy."

Maxwell laughed. "Do you t'ink she's worth risking your scalp over, *mon ami*?"

"Damn, Jacques, jist take a look at her. Wouldn't you take a run at her if you had the chance?"

"*Mais oui!*" Maxwell agreed, with another laugh. He could understand Beecher's eagerness. In fact, he had his eye on a lovely—and seemingly very interested—young woman.

At the same time, thoughts of Clydie Parkes danced about in his mind. He was still not over her; after all, it hadn't been that long. And he worried a little that he might meet one of these Crow women and find himself falling in love with her. It would be too easy to do, if even half the tales he had heard of Indian women were true. They were, if the talk of the old-hands could be believed, highly accommodating to men. They were good cooks, that was evident here tonight. And supposedly they were industrious, servile, expert at tanning hides, and more. Maxwell wasn't sure he wanted to fall into the romantic clutches of another woman just yet, no matter how enticing she might be.

He sighed. The thoughts were ridiculous. He had had more than one night with a woman since Clydie had left him heartbroken, and he had not fallen in love with any of them. Of course, they had all been whores, not supposedly warm and caring Indian women, but he thought it had built up his

resistance to a woman's ... what? Certainly not a
woman's allure. He decided it didn't matter. He
would take life as it came, just as he always had. He
would be cautious as much as he could, but if he fell
under the spell of some woman, here or elsewhere,
he would deal with it then.

Reassured, he looked up into the soft brown
eyes of the Crow woman who was serving him
another ration of well-spiced stew. He smiled, and
was rewarded with a smile in return. He took the
stew and set it beside him. As the woman turned to
leave, Maxwell grabbed the bottom of her long
buckskin dress and tugged lightly. The woman
turned back, looking expectant, he thought, and
certainly not worried.

With signs that were hesitant because of his lack
of experience in them, Maxwell let the woman know
that he was interested in her. She used sign language
in return, but her hands flew so fast that he could
not follow. He looked puzzled, and scratched his
head, shrugging to indicate he didn't understand.

The woman smiled once more, and gave the
signs more slowly, watching Maxwell's eyes to make
sure he understood as she was going along. She had
to backtrack once or twice, but finally he got the
message:

"I am Dancing Water, and I am very interested
in you, too."

Maxwell grinned and nodded. Then he signed,
his face showing nothing, "When can we be
together?"

"Soon," she signed. Then she giggled and fled,
laughing and chatting with her friends.

"Didn't take you long to latch on to a squaw, you randy old goat," Beecher said, a small note of grumbling in his voice.

"A man, 'e 'as to decide what 'e wants to do and zen did it, *mon ami*," Maxwell responded almost cheerfully.

"Well, damn you," Beecher groused. Then he grinned in apology. "I jist hope my signin's as good as yours, even as bad as that is," he added.

"If it's not, *mon ami*, you can just t'row ze woman down and get to business right zere. She'll got ze message zen, boy."

"Reckon she would," Beecher said with a laugh.

The other men, having watched Maxwell, had gotten their nerve up, and had all propositioned the young women who had been serving them. Beecher had spent enough time talking with Maxwell that he was now the only trapper who had not made a connection. He swiftly rectified that.

Soon the Crow women began returning. Taking the men by the hand, they tugged them off into the darkness, either behind some brush or trees, or into lodges.

Dancing Water took Maxwell into a tipi. After the coolness of the night, the lodge felt warm from the fire, and from the heat exuded by the two of them. They turned to each other, shyly. Though neither was inexperienced, this was, in a way, new to them. With signs, and with actions, they soon began to lose their shyness a little at a time. By the time they were naked and lying together on a bed of buffalo robes and elk hides, Maxwell realized that he wanted this woman, very much. He was downright eager to be in her, but he managed to calm himself some, wanting to make this moment last as long as possible.

Maxwell began moving his hands along her smooth flesh, awed by the sight, smell, and feel of her. She was unlike any woman he had ever been with. Yes, she had all the right parts in all the right shapes and places, yet she was so different somehow. He couldn't figure it out, and in just a few seconds, he realized it didn't matter whatsoever. She was special, and that was all there was to it. He would enjoy that specialness, and try to make himself special to her.

Maxwell should have had no worry about that, however. Dancing Water already thought of him in such terms. It was the first time she had ever seen a man with black skin, though it was not even as dark as some of her tribesmen's. His somewhat kinky hair, softened by liberal doses of bear grease, was unusual, and she found herself wanting to touch it.

Dancing Water also reveled in the feel of his hands on her, hands that were at once comfortingly familiar and hauntingly different. She hissed inwardly as Maxwell's knowing fingers covered her femaleness and lingered there, teasing, stroking, entering, and withdrawing. She moaned and ground her pelvis up against the hard heel of his hand, until she emitted a short scream of joy.

Soon Dancing Water pushed Maxwell over onto his back and climbed onto him. Her face was a mask of pleasured concentration as she wriggled her way to ecstasy again, this time accompanied to the peak by Maxwell.

When the shudders of pleasure had subsided some, Dancing Water looked down at Maxwell and smiled warmly. With her small, work-hardened hands, she signed, "Again?"

"Mais oui, mademoiselle. Mais oui!" He signed the message at the same time.

The festivities, both public and private, lasted a few days, and then the village began to settle back to normal. It was then that Maxwell finally got his men together and went to meet with the council of warriors.

"Now remember, *mes amis*," Maxwell said as he and his men were preparing to enter Great Bear's lodge, "how to found your seat at the fire, *ça va?* And when ze pipe comes around ze first time—if Great Bear offers ze pipe—to do it ze right way. *Comprendez?*"

Each man nodded tightly, nervously. They had had a heaping dose of fun since they had gotten to the village, but now came the time for business, and they were not at all certain how they would be received.

Then Beecher grinned a little. "Jist make sure you know your signin' a heap better'n you did the other day, Jacques," he said. "Them warriors ain't likely to be as forgivin' as them squaws was of misspeakin' with your hands."

Maxwell glared at Beecher, then winked once. He called for entrance. When permission was given, he said, *"Allons,"* and entered without hesitation. His eyes swept the inside of the lodge, determining where his place would be. He saw that a space had been left for him and his men to Great Bear's right. He walked around the fire, to his right until he had made his way to his seat. His men followed and took their places.

"Welcome to my village," Great Bear said. "It is good to have friends of the Trading Chief visit."

Maxwell nodded. "I am glad to be in the village of the Crow chief Great Bear," he signed. He reached into his possible sack and withdrew a piece of rolled-up buckskin that obviously contained something. He undid the leather thong that held it together, then unrolled it on the ground in front of Great Bear. "The Trading Chief sends this token of his friendship in the hope that Great Bear's village will find it to their advantage to do business with his representatives."

Maxwell sat back, sweating. He thought he had gotten everything right with his hand signs, but he could not be entirely sure. He had studied hard with the experienced men who had taught him, but there was still so much he did not know about the peculiar language, especially its nuances.

Great Bear picked up the flintlock pistol that lay before him. He looked it over closely. Then he nodded. It was a good present from Lisa. Not that it mattered. Great Bear's plan was already set. He set the gun back down on the buckskin next to the small, shiny flask of powder and the buckskin pouch of lead balls.

"It is good," Great Bear signed. "We will do business with you and your men. We owe much to the Trading Chief."

Maxwell nodded, not showing the relief that flowed over him like a flood-swollen river over its banks.

"And we ask the Trading Chief's men to winter with us in our village," Great Bear continued. "You will be safe here, and have many comforts. You all have become acquainted with some of our women," he smiled to let the men know that he did not in any way find this troublesome, "and I think they would be happy to set up lodges with you. There is time yet to hunt to make meat. We have plenty of wood and water. I think you will find life pleasant here."

"We had hoped that the wise Great Bear would allow such a thing," Maxwell said with his hands, trying to be humble. It was damn near impossible, but he thought he managed it.

Great Bear nodded curtly. He looked around the lodge, at each of the dozen or so warriors gathered there. He spoke briefly in his own language and waited to see if he got any response. The warriors, however, just nodded. Great Bear turned back to look at Maxwell. "The warriors agree that it is good that you stay."

"The generosity and hospitality of the Absaroka are known far and wide," Maxwell signed. It was only partially true, but it sounded good, and should keep him in high favor with the Crows. And being in high favor with them meant the trading would be good. That, after all, was his objective.

Still, he was beginning to have an uneasy feeling about all this. From what the old-hands had told him, the Crows, like most other Indians, liked to bargain, and like men everywhere, liked to get what they thought was the better of the deal, This had been a little too easy, he thought. The presentation of a pistol should have gotten him no more than a friendly welcome to the village and an attentive ear. Perhaps it would have been enough to get him what he had just gotten, but only after at least some negotiation.

More interesting to him was the fact that Great Bear had made the offer to have them stay in the village. Maxwell had expected to have to argue the point with Great Bear, perhaps offering some gifts or promises to get the Crow leader to acquiesce. But not only had Great Bear made the initial offer with no argument, he also offered Maxwell's small group the women with whom they had become acquainted. Again, it was not impossible for such a thing to happen, but it seemed highly suspicious to Maxwell.

Still, he had gotten what he had wanted for now, so he would let things lie for a bit. It was possible that Great Bear and his band were indeed somehow deeply indebted to Manuel Lisa and the Missouri Fur Company. And even though Great Bear didn't know Maxwell or any of his men, just the fact that they came from the company might be enough.

"It is good," Great Bear signed again. He reached out and took the long pipe one of his warriors offered him. He held it to his mouth while the warrior placed a burning stick to the tobacco in the bowl. Great Bear puffed a little until the pipe was going. He blew puffs of smoke to the four directions. Then he solemnly handed the pipe to Maxwell on his right, and watched intently.

Maxwell knew what to do, however, and followed Great Bear's example of honoring the four directions. He passed the pipe to Thornton on his right, and from there it made the rounds, first of his men, then the Crow warriors, until the pipe ended up back in Great Bear's hands. The leader nodded and handed the pipe to one warrior, who placed it reverently near Great Bear's horse-head altar.

"How is the Trading Chief?" Great Bear asked in signs.

"He is well," Maxwell lied with his hands. Having met Lisa only once, briefly, he had no idea whether the man was well or not.

They ran out of small talk then, and finally Maxwell realized it would be best if he and his men left, since Great Bear and the warriors were ignoring them anyway, talking in their own language.

Once outside, Maxwell wiped the sweat from his forehead. "'E is one strange fellow," he said.

"It *was* kind of odd in there," Beecher agreed, "and I'm damn glad to be back out here in the sunlight where I can breathe. Of course, I aim to be back in a dim ol' lodge here right quick. That li'l Singin' Flower jist can't git enough of me." He sounded mighty cocky.

"Ze reason she can't got enough of you, *mon ami*, is zat zere is not enough of you zere for her to got," Maxwell said, laughing.

All the others—except Beecher—laughed, too. Beecher grimaced, knowing he had set himself up for that, and unable at the moment to come up with a retort. "What the hell do you know anyway?" he groused as he tramped off toward where he was to meet Singing Flower.

"Well, *mes amis*," Maxwell said, "*Monsieur* Beecher may not be very good wit' ze ladies, but 'e 'as some good ideas at times. I t'ink I'll go find Dancing Water and see if she is as friendly today as she 'as been all zese other days." Pushing his concerns away for the time being, he strolled off.

Maxwell said nothing about his uneasiness for a while. Instead, he kept his suspicions to himself—and tried to make plans. He and his men rode out every day to hunt. They came back with buffalo, elk, deer, sometimes bear. Their women, who had put up their own lodges to share with their men, dried the meat, making jerky and pemmican. They kept most of the hides, too. Some were scraped free of hair and cured for use in making clothing; others were tanned with the hair on. They would be packed along with the beaver pelts for sale back in Saint Louis in the spring.

Not wanting to rely solely on trading with the Crows for their packs of beaver pelts, Maxwell had the men run their trap lines every day. He had considered trying to keep the activity hidden from the Crows, whom he worried might take exception to it, but he realized right off that Dancing Water and the other Crow women would tan the beaver pelts far better than he and his men could. In addition, the men would have no place to do the tanning away from the village. But none of the Crow leaders said anything, so Maxwell figured they didn't mind. That, too, made him somewhat suspicious. Any tribe who was planning to trade with them should have made some protest at their taking their own furs right in the band's territory like this. After all, the more pelts the company men took themselves the less they would need those traded by the Crows, which meant that the Indians would get less in the way of trade goods.

On the surface, things seemed to be going along fine. Maxwell and his men continued to be treated hospitably. They were even accorded a veneer of considerable respect. Still, Maxwell continued to have his doubts, though he still didn't know why. Making it more irritating was the fact that he did not think he could mention his suspicions to his men, mostly because he had no solid basis for those feelings. So he kept everything bottled up, which increased his tenseness. Only Dancing Water could make him forget these reservations, even if just for a while.

The little things continued to add up, however, and finally Maxwell had had enough. He had learned long ago to trust his instincts, and he had now spent too long denying his suspicions. It was time to act. He called his men into the lodge Dancing Water shared with him. Once they were all seated, wondering at what had brought this on, Maxwell said, "*Mes amis*, we are going to leave ze village."

"What?" Beecher asked, shocked and annoyed. He had become quite close to Singing Flower since being here, and he was loath to leave her. Besides, it was mighty comfortable here, living in his own lodge with Singing Flower, even if the woman did own it.

"You 'eard me, boy," Maxwell said.

"Why?" Thornton asked. He didn't particularly want to leave the village either, but he was at least willing to listen to Maxwell's reasons.

"Zat's a good question, *mon ami*," Maxwell said, rubbing his chin. He had no answer, so was reluctant to respond, but knew he had to. He simply said, "I don' trust zese Innians."

"Why not?" Lepari asked. "They've been nothing but cordial and gracious to us."

"*Oui*, zat zey 'ave. It is one of ze reasons I am suspicious of zem," Maxwell replied. "Zey 'ave been too nice, I t'ink. Remember what zose we learned from told us—to always be suspicious of Innians. And to be wary of zeir motives, *n'est-ce pas?* Well, zey 'ave been so very good to us zat I wonder if zey maybe have some end zey are not saying."

The men thought about that some, discussing it quietly among themselves. Maxwell sat patiently, waiting for them to finish. Finally, Lepari looked at Maxwell and asked, "So where do we go if we leave here?"

Maxwell shrugged. "I'm not sure, but not too far, I t'ink. We still want to trade with zese Crows. We'll find a place."

"Why don't we go find another band of Crows?" Milt Richwine asked.

"It's too late for zat," Maxwell said. "Wintair's almost here, *mes amis*. We need to find another place to wintair and put up some shelter *rapidement*—

quickly. We can't took ze time to find another band of Crows, get to meet zem, and talk zem into letting us wintair wit' zem. If zey are at all ill disposed toward us, we could find ourselves facing a hard wintair, *n'est-ce pas*?"

"When do we leave, Jacques?" Thornton asked after some moments of silence as the men digested that information.

"*Dès que possible*—as soon as possible," Maxwell said. "We 'ave enough meat. We will pull up our traps tomorrow, and be gone ze nex' morning. Is zere any argument wit' zat?" Maxwell's face made it clear he was not going to accept any argument, or protest, over his plans.

Despite that, Beecher piped up. "What about the women?" he asked, agitated.

Maxwell shrugged. "Zey will stay 'ere," he said. He glanced over at Dancing Water. He would miss her a lot. She was the best thing that had happened to him since his early days with Clydie Parkes. Her comforting nature had helped him get through the past few weeks, allowing him time to think things out, and make what he felt was a reasoned—and reasonable—decision.

"I ain't so sure I like that idea, Jacques," Beecher groused. "I got a powerful hankerin' for Singin' Flower. She's a good woman."

"*Oui*, she is zat," Maxwell agreed. "So is Dancing Water. But we can't force zem to go wit' us, take zem away from zeir people."

"Well, hell, I ain't sayin' we should *force* 'em, Jacques," Beecher said, still agitated. "But we can ask 'em if they *want* to go, can't we?"

Before Maxwell could answer, Dancing Water spoke, shocking them all. Indian women were supposed to keep their silence around the men, especially when business was being discussed. Indeed, they were not supposed to say anything in public—and this constituted public at the moment—unless they were spoken to first. The men had not understood her, since she had spoken in her own language, but they all turned to look at her.

"I will go with you, Black Skinned Chief," she said with signs, using the appellation she had given Maxwell.

"Are you sure?" Maxwell asked in signs.

Dancing Water nodded.

Maxwell turned back to his men. "You boys can ask your women if zey would like to come wit' us. But," he added sternly, "if zey say no, zat is zat. If I learn zat you tried to force zem to say yes, I will deal wit' you in most unpleasant ways, *mes amis*. *Comprendez?*"

His six subordinates nodded.

"Zen go ask. Just told zem we are leaving ze village. Don' told zem why, *ça va?*" As he watched his men head out into the cold night air, Maxwell sat there, thinking hard. Something about what had just occurred bothered him, but he could not figure it out. He was reaching for the coffee pot to refill his cup when it hit him. Still kneeling, and bending forward, he glanced over his shoulder at Dancing Water, who was working quietly on beading a shirt she planned to trade.

"Zut!" he muttered and rose and went to her. She sensed him coming and stood to meet him. He stopped a foot away from her. "I thought you didn't understand my language," he said with signs. His face was hard.

"I don't," Dancing Water responded in kind. She suddenly looked worried.

"Then how did you know what me and my men were discussing?" he asked, his choppy arm and hand movements showing his annoyance.

Dancing Water's face blanched, but she tried immediately to hide her consternation. "I didn't," she said in signs.

"*Menteuse!* Liar!" Maxwell snapped. "Now tell me ze trut', *une peau ze vache*—you bitch."

Dancing Water's face turned downcast and she would not look at him. Then her features hardened. "I speak and understand English," she said, her voice harsh and suddenly ugly. "And your other language, too."

"*Francais?*" Maxwell asked, surprised.

"*Oui.*"

Maxwell stood there, trying to decide what all this meant, but he could come up with no answer. All he could do was ask, "*Porquoi m'as-tu menti?* Why'd you lie to me?"

"Great Bear ask me to," Dancing Water responded, looking defiantly at Maxwell. "He's my uncle." Her English was no worse than Maxwell's, but it was quite heavily accented.

"*Porquoi*—why?"

Dancing Water shrugged. "He just ask me, so I do it. He not tell me why."

"You know anyt'ing else you 'aven't told me?" Maxwell asked. He didn't like this development. All it did was increase his suspicions that something was afoot in the Crow village, and that it likely did not bode well for him and his men.

"*Non*," Dancing Water answered flatly.

Maxwell didn't believe her, but since he could not prove otherwise, he nodded in acceptance. He went back to the fire, ruminating on what he had just learned. He did not—could not again—trust Dancing Water, so he considered leaving her here when he and the others rode out. Then he realized that if she did know something else, or was aware of some plot against his group, she might be valuable to have—as long as they all watched what was said in her presence.

That led him to wondering if the other women had also been lying. He could not do anything about it tonight anyway, so he tried to put it out of his mind, which proved to be futile. It made for a night of poor sleep, and he awoke in a considerably cantankerous humor. After a perfunctory breakfast, served by a tight-lipped and peevish Dancing Water, he headed outside. He was glad to see that, despite her petulance, she had saddled his horse. He gathered up his men, and they rode out. All but Maxwell seemed to be in fine spirits.

When they were a mile or so outside the village, and had already checked several of their traps, Maxwell called a halt. They tied their horses to some trees, and then hunkered down in the protection of some thick brush, which blunted the biting wind somewhat. It was obvious that winter wasn't far off. There was silence for a bit, except for the rush of the wind, and the clattering of the aspen leaves as they scuttled across the ground.

"You boys t'ink zere was anyt'ing strange about our little parley last night?" Maxwell finally asked.

All the men but one shook their heads, some with more confidence than others.

Pete Lepari was the odd man out. "Somethin' bothers me about that, Jacques," he said hesitantly, worrying that his companions would make fun of him. "But I can't figure it out." He chewed on his fingernails, already gnawed to the quick. "Somethin' wasn't right, though. I know that much," he said, taking a brief respite from nibbling at his nails.

"Zat is true, *mon ami*. Now t'ink, all of you. What 'appened during ze parley zat was unusual, eh?"

They all sat a minute before the usually very quiet George Stroud said, "Dancin' Water. She said she would come with us."

"So?" Beecher demanded. "That don't mean nothin' more than she's got a hankerin' for that goat-lovin' ol' curmudgeon she's sharin' her robes with, though God only knows why an otherwise sane woman'd do such a thing."

"No, it does mean somethin'," Lepari put in, thinking he was on the right track, and trying to solidify the ethereal thought he had had. "Yeah, dammit, she couldn't have said she'd come with us if she didn't understand English!" he said, relieved that he had pulled it all together like that.

"*Exactement, mon ami. Exactement.*"

The men were even more stunned now than they had been the night before when Dancing Water had actually had the audacity to speak during their discussion.

"Now," Maxwell said, "zat might not be too bad

a t'ing. Maybe she was just playin' a joke on us, *mes amis*. But on ze other 'and, it might mean zat she knows a lot more. Maybe even somet'ing zat could be bad for us, *n'est-ce pas?*"

"So do we leave her behind, Jacques?" Beecher asked. He felt bad for Maxwell, but on the other hand, as long as he could bring Singing Flower, he was all right.

"Maybe we should leave all the women behind," Lepari said thoughtfully.

"Like hell," Beecher snapped. "I ain't leavin' Singin' Flower jist 'cause Jacques's woman's been lyin' to him."

"Would you use your head for somethin' other than a place to rest your hat, you dumb bastard," Lepari snarled back.

"I don't think he can do that," Richwine said in his sonorous voice. He smiled.

"Maybe not," Lepari said. "But if he can't, we'll have to help him do it." He paused to chew on his nails again for a few moments. "Don't you see, Lucius," he continued, "that if Dancin' Water was lyin' about this, then all our women might be lyin' about it, too?"

"So?" Beecher was being sulky, which he often was when things did not go his way. "What's the harm?"

"Like Jacques said," Thornton noted, "maybe it don't mean nothin'. But maybe it means a lot."

"Like what?" Beecher groused. "Are they gonna attack us or somethin'?"

"Ze women, no," Maxwell said. "But ze men, maybe yes."

"Why in hell would the Crows attack us, dammit?" Beecher was growing angrier by the moment. "They been mighty congenial since we been there, they're friends with Mister Lisa, and they've dealt with Mister Lisa's company for a long time now. It's ridiculous to think they'd attack us just because your woman pretended she couldn't understand our talk."

"I must confess zat I 'ave no reason to t'ink zey would attack us, *mon ami*," Maxwell said with a shrug. "But zey might want our trade goods wit'out 'aving to pay for zem wit' beaver pelts. Maybe zey don't 'ave any beaver plews, as our experienced friend John Peabody calls zem, eh? Did you evair t'ink of zat, *monsieur?*"

"No, dammit, I didn't, and you goddamn well know it, too, you son of a bitch," Beecher grumbled.

"So, Jacques, do we leave the women behind when we go?" Lepari asked. He would rather bring Lodge Fire than leave her in the village, but not at the cost of his hair.

"*Mais non,*" Maxwell said firmly. "We take zem. After all, if zere is a plot by ze Crows to do somet'ing to us, ze women might know about it, and we might be able to learn of it before it 'appens, *n'est-ce pas?*"

The men nodded, knowing that Maxwell would beat the information out of the women if he thought that was necessary.

"Until zen, we must watch what we say in front of zem, at all times. *Comprendez?*"

Again the men nodded.

"Just one more t'ing, *mes amis,*" Maxwell added.

"Since ze women expect us to leave in ze morning, and maybe 'ave told ze warriors about it, we will pull out today. As soon as we can finish pulling our traps and get back to ze camp. We'll ride in zere, tell ze women we are leaving now, and set zem to work. While zey are doing so, I will go tell Great Bear about it. Zat way zey will not 'ave time to change zeir plans if zey were t'inking of doing somet'ing to us before we left tomorrow. Ça va?"

Maxwell's six men were in agreement, and planned to hurry as much as possible so they could get as early a start as could be managed.

18

Great Bear was not at all pleased at this sudden turn of events, and he expressed his dissatisfaction with a furious barrage of angry hand and arm movements. Maxwell sat there and let the Crow leader get it all out of his system before saying simply, with signs, "We feel we're being a burden on your people, Great Bear. And we need some elbow room so we don't have to worry about violating any of your rules."

They were lies, of course, and not particularly good ones at that, but Maxwell didn't care. He was leaving this afternoon, no matter how much Great Bear objected to it. While he didn't say it aloud, Maxwell had told himself silently that the only way he would stay in the village was if Great Bear's warriors prevented him and his men from leaving.

"You're no burden here," Great Bear signed, trying to look concerned that Maxwell would feel that way about his people. "We have plenty of food for the long winter, and your men have made much of their own meat. You are taking nothing from us."

"But we are not giving anything back, either," Maxwell responded. "It's a custom among my people to pay back such generosity as Great Bear's people have shown us. And we can't do that. Not until spring, anyway."

"If you leave today, I will be insulted," Great Bear signed. "And all my people will be insulted. It is a custom among the Absaroka to treat our guests even better than the members of our own band. For a visitor to reject that hand of kindness is a great insult to us."

Maxwell had no idea whether Great Bear was telling the truth or not. He suspected that there was at least a little truth to it, but not much. It still didn't matter to him. All Great Bear's protests were doing was aggravating him. While he was preparing to respond, an idea hit him, and he had to fight back a smile. "I mean no insult, Great Bear, and when I return in the spring to trade, there will be many presents for the great chief of the Absaroka," he signed.

At the same time, however, he spoke aloud, using a quiet, even tone, "We're leaving 'ere today, and you can't stop us, you ill-humored, skunk-'umping son of a bitch. *Un moche, connard merdier*— you ugly, stupid shit pile."

Maxwell had to fight hard to keep from showing his elation at seeing that Great Bear knew quite well the words he had spoken. The Crow leader tried to hide it, but Maxwell saw the ever-so-brief look of recognition and realization in Great Bear's eyes. And the even briefer hate that had burned there. *Got you, you deceiving bastard*, Maxwell thought.

Great Bear sighed, as if finally convinced that Maxwell and his men were determined to leave. He eyed Maxwell carefully, trying to see if the trader had caught on that he knew what Maxwell had said aloud. He thought he had disguised it well, and thought Maxwell hadn't caught on, by the looks of him. "If you think you must go," he said with signs, "then I can't stop you. But you are always welcome in Great Bear's village."

"Thank you, great chief," Maxwell signed. In his head he added, *you walking pile of buffalo droppings.* "Do you know of a good place where we might go?" he asked in signs.

"Three miles northeast along Wolf Creek there is a place we have used before. Like this one, it has plenty of wood and water, trees to break the raging of the wind, grass for your horses. You will be comfortable there. And close enough that if the Blackfeet or some other enemy bothers you we can come to help quickly."

"Again, I am in your debt, Great Bear," said. He stood and headed out. His men were nervously waiting for him at their lodges, watching their women taking down the tipis and packing their belongings. Maxwell had made it clear before he went to see Great Bear that he wanted the women watched closely, so that none of them could sneak off to report on things. The men, angry that they might have been deceived, and wary about the possibility of having the seemingly friendly Crows turn against them, had done an excellent job of it. In fact, the women, hoping to stall long enough so that they couldn't leave that day, worked at a molasseslike pace, until the men cajoled, ordered, and then threatened them to speed up their work.

Since all their lodges were clustered together, only two or three of the men were needed to keep an eye on the women as they worked, so Maxwell took Richwine, Thornton, and Lepari with him. They would load their trade goods while the others kept the work moving with the lodges.

It was still early afternoon when they rode out under another light snowfall. They headed northeast along Wolf Creek. But less than a mile from the village, Maxwell turned them roughly north-westward, away from the creek. He noted with a little satisfaction that at least two of the women seemed irritated by the maneuver.

Nightfall overtook them before they reached the Tongue River, but they did find a patch of pines and brush where they could make their camp. "Zere will be no need for ze lodges zis night," he said to Dancing Water. There was no longer a pretense between them and the others that she did not speak English. The other women, however, were either unable to speak English or were still faking it well. "Just a couple of fires for ze cooking and to keep warm. Ze trees and brush will be enough cover."

Dancing Water nodded and gave the orders to the other women in Crow. Maxwell and the men began to unsaddle their horses and unload their supplies and trade goods off the other horses.

"Where're we headed, Jacques?" Lepari asked as they worked.

"I don' know for sure," Maxwell admitted.

"Why'd you turn us away from the creek?" Thornton asked. He worried that they might get lost without it or some other river to guide them.

"Great Bear told me of a good place to wintair— maybe t'ree miles nort'east of ze village."

"Then why are we headin' north?" Beecher asked. He was vigorously brushing down one of the horses.

"Do I trust *Monsieur* Great Bear? Eh? *Mais non!* So I will take us nort' for a little, zen west, well nort' of ze village. Once we are past zat camp, we will look for a spot to wintair."

"Sounds reasonable to me," Thornton said. The others agreed with him.

"You just bein' cautious, Jacques?" Lepari asked. "Or did you learn somethin' in your parley with Great Bear today?"

"I learned a little somet'ing, yes." Maxwell stopped brushing his horse and leaned a forearm on the animal. "I learned zat 'e is another sneaky bastard. *Mais oui.* He also knows English and *Francais.*"

"You sure?" Beecher asked.

"*Oui.*"

"That ol' son of a bitch," Beecher said. "Damn, it don't pay to trust a one of these red men, does it?"

"If Great Bear and his band are a good example of ze Innians out here, zen I would say no, it's not a good t'ing to trust zem. I certainly trust zat band less every day. I still don' know if Great Bear plans to come against us, but ze more I see 'im act, ze more I t'ink it's likely. So we go somewhere he doesn't expect us to. 'E'll find us, *bien sûr*, but 'e'll 'ave to look for us for at least a little while. We can use ze time to get ready for ze cunning old bastard."

"That sounds reasonable," Beecher said.

They got an early start in the morning and pushed hard. At one point, from a ledge on a small mountainous upcropping, they could see the smoke from the village well to the south. It wasn't easily seen, but with some squinting and undivided attention, they did spot the low pall of smoke. They pushed on.

As the day progressed, Maxwell turned them a little more northwest, trying to angle toward the Tongue River. As dusk approached, they made camp by a small stream, and the next day followed the stream. It eventually brought them to the Yellowstone. Maxwell sighed with relief. They followed the river westward again, heading higher into the mountains. Maxwell wished he had known before that it was so close. It would have saved them some traveling, but that could not be helped now.

In midafternoon, Maxwell found a spot that seemed a reasonable place to spend the winter. It was much like the place where Great Bear's Crow band had their village, though this valley was considerably higher in the mountains. "Zis will do, *mes amis*," Maxwell said. "Dancing Water, you and ze other women get ze lodges up and fires started. *Vite*. Zere is much to be done."

A scowl distorted Dancing Water's beautiful face briefly. She and Maxwell had been mighty testy with each other since Maxwell had discovered that she understood him and his men. She had grown even more distant when Maxwell had turned away from the wintering spot Great Bear had directed them to. And she didn't like being ordered about in such a way either. But she sighed. She was stuck here for the time being, so she figured she might as well make the best of it. Things would change for the better soon, of that she was sure.

Over the next day or two, she talked with the other women, quietly, though with a note of urgency and command in her voice. She quickly convinced the others that they must begin to treat their men better. It would win them better treatment and, with some luck, make the men relax their guard.

The men were suspicious at first when the women began acting as friendly and warm as they had been in the village, but they swiftly got used to the idea, believing that, now that they had stopped traveling and had their own camp, the women could relax and let their usual kind natures shine through.

Maxwell, the most wary among them, refused for several days to let himself be lulled into a feeling of security, but then Dancing Water got through to him. She had been quite solicitous at night in the robes, and he had enjoyed it, though he had managed to still keep himself aloof. She finally asked him straight out, "What's wrong, Black Skinned Chief?"

"You know what's ze problem is, woman," Maxwell answered flatly.

"*Oui*," Dancing Water responded sadly. "I deceive you. That's bad, I know. Can I make me good to you again?"

Maxwell shrugged. It wasn't bad enough that she had deceived him, and that he thought she might be in on some plot of her people against him and his men, but he had fallen in love with her early on, and thoughts of the anguish Clydie had left him in were ever present. He was certain that if he gave himself too deeply to Dancing Water, she, too, would end up hurting his heart. It was better to keep himself distant from her, while still enjoying carnal pleasures with her, and eating her cooking and letting her tend him.

But as the days passed, and nothing untoward happened, Maxwell relented some. Out of sight of the village, and with the Crow women being so eager to please, the men relaxed. Even Maxwell let his guard down more. It was not that he trusted Dancing Water implicitly now, it was more that he had been lulled into thinking that in such a realtively comfortable, serene setting, nothing could happen. There had been no sign of Crow warriors about, and Maxwell finally decided that his imagination had been overactive back in the village. He didn't regret leaving the Crow camp, since he realized that if he hadn't, he would still be plagued with thoughts of potential trouble. Here he could relax his mind as well as his body.

As they awoke one morning a week after they had made their own camp, George Stroud hurried through the chill to Maxwell's lodge and entered. He grabbed a cup of coffee as he squatted by the fire. "Yellow Crow's gone," he said flatly.

"Are you certain she didn't just go down to ze rivair for some water?" Maxwell asked. He was a little concerned. "Or back into ze bushes to relieve herself?"

"Her pony's gone, too."

"She give you any indication she 'ad somet'ing to do? Some special task or somet'ing?"

"Nope. Not a goddamn word."

"Did she seem to be un'appy being 'ere?"

"Nope. I thought things was goin' just goddamn fine. When I roused myself this mornin', the fire was burned down some, meanin' she never stoked it up. I went out to look for her, and couldn't find her. Then I checked the horses, and her pony was gone."

"*Zut! Allors!*" Maxwell muttered. He looked at Dancing Water. "You know anyt'ing about zis, woman?" he asked roughly. When she hesitated, he said, "Don' lie to me again, *tu putain!*" he snapped.

Dancing Water nodded. "She want to go home."

"Why now? And why sneak out like zis, eh?" Maxwell's eyes were narrowed in anger. He cursed himself inwardly for having let his guard down so much.

"She . . . she . . . "

"Zat *putain*, she went to told Great Bear and ze warriors where we are, *non?*" Maxwell asked, his voice furious.

Dancing Water hung her head, but did not say anything.

"*Zut! Ce cradingue un pot à tabac une petite*

putain—that dirty, dumpy little whore," Maxwell snarled. He swung toward Stroud. "Saddle yourself an 'orse, *mon ami*, and chase after zat *putain*. *Vite*. Ran 'er down, and when you caught 'er, kill 'er."

"I don't know as if I could kill a woman, Jacques," Stroud said indecisively. "Not one I been layin' with regular for some weeks."

"*Zut!* Zen ran 'er down and bring 'er back 'ere. I'll take care of zat *salope*—bitch. Now go. *Allez! Vite, vite!*"

Stroud hurried out, running across the light coating of snow toward the horses. The other men saw his flight and, confused, began drifting toward Maxwell's lodge.

"What the hell's wrong with George?" Lepari asked.

Maxwell explained it in a few short, profane sentences. Then he added, "You boys better stay wit' your women for now. Keep zem from running away."

Stroud galloped past them on his way out of the village. His face was white from cold, fear, and anger. He was glad for the little snow that had fallen overnight. He would be able to follow Yellow Crow's tracks easily, though it shouldn't matter. She would be heading for Great Bear's village, and Stroud knew in what direction that lay.

Back in the camp, Maxwell had paid no heed to Stroud's departure. "Tie ze damn women up if you 'ave to, but keep zem 'ere."

"Shit, I say we let 'em go if they're of a mind to," Beecher said. He felt betrayed, even though it hadn't been Singing Flower who had gone to pass the word of their whereabouts. He was the one who had been so insistent on taking the women with them when they left the village, so he figured he should take at least some of the blame.

"Ze Crows, zey might not be so eager to attack us if we 'ave zeir women. Or maybe zey won' care, I don' know. Who can tell wit' zese savages." He paused, then added, "And be ready to fight, *mes amis*, eh? It might come to zat."

An hour after he had left, Stroud came thundering back into camp. The men in the camp heard the commotion and boiled out of their lodges to see what they faced. Close on Stroud's heels were about two dozen Crow warriors, led by Great Bear and Blue Smoke.

19

Just as the men tumbled out of their lodges, three arrows thudded into Stroud's back. He fell sideways, tried to right himself in the saddle, but then flopped to the ground, bouncing several times before coming to a stop. He left a trail of red snow and broken arrow shafts behind him.

Maxwell immediately saw how outmanned he and his men were, and he knew they could not hope to win a fight. *"Cache, mes amis!"* he bellowed. *"Vite! Vite!* Run for cover." He dropped to one knee and brought his rifle up and fired. He had been hoping to get a shot at Great Bear, but the chief was not to be seen. Instead, Maxwell dropped a warrior he didn't really know. He jumped up and ran, heading for cover in the thick brush along the river. He reloaded as he ran, expecting any minute to feel the sharp sting of an arrow piercing his flesh.

A little to his left and slightly ahead of him, Maxwell saw Nils Nordgren go down, an arrow in the back of his left thigh. Maxwell veered toward his wounded friend. He slipped to a stop at Nordgren's

side, almost falling in the snow. He grabbed
Nordgren under the left arm and jerked him to his
feet through sheer strength. "Can you run, *mon
ami*?" he asked urgently.

"Yah!" With rifle in his right hand, and his left
arm around Maxwell's shoulders for balance,
Nordgren hobbled swiftly the last few yards to the
thickets. They both stopped, puffing hard from their
run.

Maxwell looked out over his camp. The Crows
had stopped chasing the men and were ransacking
the camp. He also saw Dancing Water talking
animatedly with Great Bear. He wasn't sure at this
distance, but she seemed agitated rather than elated.
He figured that perhaps she had just been told she
was not going to get as large a share of the plunder
as she thought she deserved.

"*Zut!*" he mumbled. He was heartsick for
several reasons. For one, he had been betrayed by a
woman again. For another, it was just plain galling
that he and his men had been routed so easily. Plus
he had lost one man, and had at least one more
wounded. But most of all, he felt sick because it was
obvious he was about to lose everything of the
company's—horses, traps, supplies, trade goods. He
hated himself for having been such a poor company
employee. The company had given him a chance
few other men of his color got, and here he had
failed utterly, miserably. Even if he got out of all this
alive, he could not ever face any of the company's
men again. Not unless he got back all that had been
lost and a lot more besides. He vowed then and
there that he would expend every effort in doing

so—or he would die in the attempt. He also promised himself that he would kill as many Crows as he could in the doing.

"You ready to move, *mon ami*?" he asked Nordgren.

The small, slender Swede nodded.

The two of them moved on deeper into the brush, Maxwell helping Nordgren hobble along. Some yards later, someone called out, "Jacques, Nils, over here."

Maxwell looked and spotted Lepari for a brief moment. He headed that way. They had to push through some thorny brush, but they came out in an opening just about big enough for the men. All the others were there, looking frightened and dejected.

"Those heathens comin' after us?" Beecher asked. All his cockiness was gone now. He was just a scared young man who saw little hope of having a future.

"*Non*. Zey are more interested in our plunder. I t'ink zat's what zey wanted all along." He helped Nordgren sit.

"Then why didn't they just kill us and scalp us in their village?" Thornton asked. He, too, was scared to death, and worried that he was going to have his young life cut short at any moment. But he had some faith left in himself, and in Maxwell.

"I don' know, *mon ami*," Maxwell said. He felt exhausted, though he had woken from sleep less than two hours ago. "I t'ink maybe zey t'ink if zey do zat and ze company finds out about it, zen ze company won' trade wit' zem. Or worse, will send men to hunt zem down."

"Seems plausible," Thornton said. He felt like a fool for having even asked.

Maxwell shrugged. "Or maybe zey were waiting for us to trap more beavair over ze wintair." He sighed. "It don' really matter now, eh?" He knelt alongside Nordgren. "Lay down on your belly, *mon ami*," Maxwell said to Nordgren. "I 'ave to seen about your wound."

"You von't cut my leg off, vill you?" Nordgren asked worriedly.

"What ze 'ell am I going to done wit' a one-legged Swede, eh, *mon ami*? If ze leg is zat bad, you'll die because I don' 'ave ze time or ze inclination to done anyt'ing else. *Ça va?*"

"You're a cheerful son of a bitch, ain't you?" Nordgren responded before he rolled over onto his belly.

Maxwell swiftly slit the back of Nordgren's pants and looked at the wound. He jiggled the arrow shaft a little to see how deeply imbedded it was. "It don' seem too bad, Nils," he commented. "But I must cut ze arrowhead out."

"Can't you yoost pull it out?" Nordgren asked.

"Remember what *Monsieur* Peabody told us? About how ze Innians use ze arrowheads zat cause more trouble coming out zan going in? If I pull zis one out and it's one of zem arrowheads, you'll be in worse shape zan you are now."

"All right, for chrissakes, cut it out," Nordgren snapped.

"Some of you boys 'old 'im down. One of you stick a piece of clot' in 'is mout' to keep 'im quiet." When that was done, Maxwell held the arrow shaft tightly in one hand. Then he took his knife and made three quick incisions deep into the muscle of the leg. The moves elicited muffled grunts from the gagged Nordgren, and the Swede's legs jerked a little. Maxwell yanked the arrow shaft and it came free. He tossed the bloody thing aside, wishing he had a fire. It'd be so much easier to just slap hot steel to the wound to cauterize it. But he didn't, so he reached into his possible sack, pulled out a piece of sinew and a needle. He threaded the needle and put a few hurried stitches into the flesh, just enough to crudely close the wound. He tied the sinew off and cut the excess. Then he pulled the bandanna—the one he often wore wrapped around his head—from his neck and used it to bind the wound.

"*Je suis fini, monsieurs*," Maxwell said as he rocked back on his heels.

The others helped Nordgren into a sitting position and then left him, going to squat around the small brush arena.

"So, *mon ami*, 'ow are you feeling?" Maxwell asked.

"Yoost grand, Jacques," Nordgren said with a grimace. His leg felt as if it were on fire, and his head was a little woozy, but he was determined not to let it slow anyone down. If they had to be on the move, he was planning to go.

"*Bon*," Maxwell said flatly.

The men were silent for a while as they sat and listened to the commotion emanating from their camp. Finally Lepari said, "Sounds like those boys are havin' themselves a right fine time." He went back to chewing on what little was left of his fingernails.

Maxwell nodded.

"So what do we do now, Jacques?" Thornton asked.

"I t'ink we need to got away from 'ere," Maxwell responded. "I t'ink zem Crows are too damn close."

"Amen," Beecher breathed.

"And I t'ink zem Crows will came after us sooner or later. I don' want to be around 'ere when zey do," Maxwell said. He looked at Nordgren. "Can you walk at all, Nils?" he asked.

"Yah," Nordgren said strongly. "I might be a little slow, but you boys yoost keep going. I'll catch up when I can."

"*Mais non!*" Maxwell snapped. "We are still employees of Monsieur Lisa's fur company, eh? And so we will stuck together. Is zat agreed?" He looked from one man to the next.

Each, in turn, nodded. Several had thought of arguing, but when they saw the look on Maxwell's face—and when they thought about their own pride and manliness, none could go against Maxwell.

"*Bon*. Now let's go. *Allons*," Maxwell said. As he went to help Nordgren up, Maxwell felt someone tug on his arm.

"I'll help Nils," Richwine said. "Him and me're friends, and friends help friends."

Maxwell nodded. Milt Richwine was an odd sort of fellow. Big, brawny, with a face that looked as if it had been fashioned out of old tree bark. Despite his rough-hewn, even ugly, exterior he was a polite and well-mannered man who did his work without complaint. He never asked for help, but often offered it. All in all, Maxwell was glad to have him along, especially now. If Nordgren faltered at all, Richwine was big enough and strong enough to lug his friend across half the Rocky Mountains, if necessary.

"I will lead ze way, *mes amis*," Maxwell said. "*Monsieur* Lepari, would you brought up ze rear and watch for ze savages, *s'il vous plaît*?"

Lepari, who was gnawing on his fingernails, as usual, simply nodded, blue eyes alert.

Maxwell turned and forced his way through the brush, holding back branches when he could, until they were out of their small haven. Then he led them upriver, trying to find the path with the fewest obstacles. He wanted to make time in getting away from here, if he could, and he wanted to make it as easy on Nordgren as possible. Since he was so certain that the Crows would be after them, he wanted his men to stay at least somewhat fresh in case they needed to fight again.

Around noon, Maxwell called a halt. Nordgren was exhausted, and the other men looked as if they needed a rest. He chose a spot with a little beach at the river, just down a short bank. It would make it easy for all to drink their fill from the Tongue. He wished they had some food.

As they sat there, Beecher, who was directly on Maxwell's left, tugged the shoulder of the leader's buckskin shirt and pointed to a deer less than twenty yards away. Maxwell shook his head. "We can't afford to made ze noise of shooting," he whispered.

"Like hell," Beecher hissed. "If them Crows're still back at our camp, they'll never hear it. If they're close enough to hear it, we're in deep goddamn trouble anyway."

Maxwell thought it over, uncertain.

"Look," Beecher said in an urgent whisper, "if we're gonna git away from those fractious savages out there, we got to have our strength. And for that we need meat. Look at the men, Jacques, they're near done in."

One glance at his crew was all Maxwell needed. He nodded, and then whispered, "Don' you miss, you son of a bitch."

"Me? Never happen, boy." Beecher was cocky, but he was an excellent shot. He dropped the doe easily.

As soon as he did, Maxwell said, "Pierre, you and Henri go out zere and butcher zat deer. *Vite!* One of you do ze butchering and ze other keep watch. You others 'ere, watch for Crows, eh?"

Ten minutes later the men were gorging on raw, bloody deer meat. None minded that it was not cooked. Right now they just wanted the meat's strength-giving nourishment. Afterward, some of the men nodded off. Maxwell did so, too, having learned aboard Lafitte's ship how beneficial it was to nap when one could. You could never be sure when you would be called upon to go into action, and being tired would slow a man down, often fatally. Maxwell could drop off at a moment's notice and wake just as quickly.

He woke himself an hour later. He stood and stretched. He felt rested and ready to move on. Even his gloom had lifted a little bit. He went around to his men, shaking each one gently, rousing them. When they were all awake, Maxwell decided that they all looked better for the brief rest. "You boys ready to move on again?" he asked.

Everyone nodded, and Maxwell led the little procession off along the river.

Dusk was creeping up on them before they halted again. Maxwell had stopped and was looking around carefully. He nodded. "Zis is as far as we go, *mes amis*," he said.

"Don't look like much," Beecher said. He wasn't complaining, really, just commenting.

"Zat may be true, Lucius," Maxwell said without rancor, "but it's a defensible spot. Wit' any luck, ze Crows, zey won' come for us for a little while yet. Zat will give us time to dig in. Zen we will 'ave a big surprise for zem when zey do find us, eh?"

"After this mornin', I never thought I'd want to see another Crow again in all my days," Beecher said. "But now, I'm lookin' forward to it. Those red skunks are due a heapin' dose of payin' back, as far as this ol' boy's concerned."

Maxwell still felt like hell because of all that had happened, and now he felt like a failure. But Beecher's words and expression of determination—matched by the looks in the other men's eyes—were heartening. He almost could believe a little that they might get their plunder back, and still somehow make a successful season out of this disaster.

"Zat's ze spirit, *mon ami*," he said, clapping a hand on Beecher's shoulder. "Zose Crows do 'ave a lot to pay for, *bien sûr*." He looked around at his men, proud of them, and letting it show. They had started out as novices, little more than boys, scared of everything. Now they were men, toughened by the harshness of life in this deadly land. "Now, let's get to work before zose Crows come sneaking up and stick zeir lances up our asses, *ça va?*"

There really wasn't all that much to do. There were some deadfalls which they built up with dirt, wood, and rocks. Maxwell ordered Beecher out to hunt, and had Thornton gather as much firewood as he could. Once a fire was built, Thornton went back to helping the others with the fortifications. Nordgren, who was in considerable pain now, and looking spent, sat near the fire with what small hunks of lead the men had, a small pot, and a bullet mold, making rifle and pistol balls.

Maxwell slipped away from the others and headed back down the trail he and his men had just taken. He walked swiftly, surely. He decided he had spent enough time feeling poorly about himself. He would do what needed to be done to retrieve the company's property and to restore his pride, it was that simple. If he ran into the Crows now, he would duck into the trees and brush and let them try to root him out. After a few minutes he began to trot. As a boy back at Falling Oaks, he had been a good runner. He wasn't sure he still had the capacity for it, but he wanted to see.

Jogging, he made it back as far as their noon stopping place. He saw no sign of the Crows, which was a relief. While he was prepared to face them whenever and wherever he could, he wanted it to be on his terms, if at all possible, which this wouldn't be.

He rested there briefly, and began trotting back toward where his men were. Half a mile before getting there, he shot a small deer. He slung his rifle across his back by the leather strap, then he hefted the deer over his shoulders and walked on. It was almost dark when he walked into the camp.

"Where the hell have you been, dammit?" Beecher asked, irritated.

Maxwell told them after dropping the deer carcass.

"Well, I guess that's all right then," Beecher said, almost pouting.

Maxwell laughed a little. "*Merci, le pére* Beecher," he said.

Beecher had also been successful at his hunting, and some moose meat was roasting over the fire. Maxwell sat and cut off a generous hunk with his knife and ate. When he had had his fill, he wiped his greasy hands on his filthy outfit, and then said, "Zis is my plan, *mes amis*, so pay attention."

20

"I t'ink about zis all ze time I was gone zis afternoon," Maxwell said. "And I t'ink it's ze best t'ing to do. I will 'ead back toward ze camp we 'ad. From zere, I will made ze effort to draw ze Crows away from you."

"You're goddamn deranged, Jacques," Thornton said.

"Many 'ave said zat. Maybe it's even true. No matter, though. I am going to do zis, and zat's zat."

"But . . ." Beecher started.

"*Zut!* Don' you understand ze English, *mon ami*? I am ze leader of zis venture, *n'est-ce pas*? I make ze decisions, you boys follow zem. Zat is all zere is to it."

"You're worse'n my pa, for chrissakes," Beecher said.

Maxwell shrugged. "You men are to wait 'ere for a while after I leave. Maybe 'alf a day. Zat should be long enough. Zen you try to make it back to our wintair camp and see if zere is anyt'ing left to recover. Take whatever you can, *mes amis*. Be careful, though, eh? I 'ope to get all ze Crows away from zere, but I t'ink zey will left a few of ze warriors behind, so expect at least a little resistance."

The men thought that over a bit, then Lepari said, "So, Jacques, just what do we do once we recover all this plunder the Crows'll leave behind?"

"You will 'ead back to ze company's post, *mes amis*," Maxwell said simply.

"And you, you dumb bastard, will be lyin' out here as worm food because you want to be a goddamn hero," Thornton snapped.

"Maybe, *mon ami*, maybe. But I don' plan on letting zose damn Crows catch me. I got plans for zem *dégonflés*—chickens," Maxwell said. "Zey 'ave much to paid for, *mes amis*, and I t'ink I am ze one who will make zem pay."

"Piss on you, dammit," Beecher said. "You send us straggle-assin' back out of the mountains, and across the goddamn freezin' plains in the dead of winter, whilst you set up here pickin' off some devilish ol' Crows? I reckon that don't sit well with me, boy."

Maxwell grinned, but there was little humor to it. "Zen see if you can get most of our plunder and come back 'ere. Zis way, when ze Crows get tired of chasing me, and zey find you, you will 'ave a place to defend yourselves well."

The others remained skeptical and showed it.

"Look, *mes amis*, all I want to do is get zem damn Crows away from our wintair camp long enough for you to retrieve most of our pelts, supplies, and trade goods and get back 'ere where we can make a stand."

"What makes you think they haven't headed back to their village with all our things already?" Lepari asked.

"I don't know zat. I just 'ope zey 'ave spent so much time going t'rough everyt'ing zat zey got caught in ze dark and spent ze night zere."

"Even if they did," Thornton said, "they'll likely leave come first light."

"Not if I am zere at first light," Maxwell said, "and cause zem enough annoyance zat most of zem come chasing after me. Zen all ze goods—and ze 'orses—will still be zere for you to take back."

"By Jesus, I think this dumb ol' fart has come up with an actual plan," Beecher said, feigning amazement. "Damn thing might even come close to workin', too."

"Oh, it will work, *mon ami*," Maxwell said with a small smile, "if you can 'old up your end of t'ings."

"Don't you worry about that, old man," Beecher said cockily. Most of his natural arrogance had returned in a hurry, and he even looked forward to fighting the Crows again. Only this time he did not plan to be surprised by the Indians.

Maxwell took another piece of meat and chewed it slowly. "You boys better get some rest soon, eh? You 'ave a long day tomorrow."

"What about you, Jacques?" Thornton asked. "If you're plannin' on being back at our old camp come first light, you'll have to do a heap of travelin' tonight."

"*Oui*. But I will take ze nap soon. Zen I will go. I will be all right, *mon ami*, don't you t'ink differently." When he finished the piece of meat, Maxwell shuffled his back against a rock until he was almost comfortable, then he dozed off.

Judging by the stars and the moon, Maxwell estimated he had been asleep for a little over an hour and a half. He rose and stoked up the fire just a little. There was still some meat there. He heated it and ate, wishing there was coffee. When he had his fill, he pulled his blanket coat closer around him, checked his rifle and shooting supplies, and headed out.

The wind was blowing, as it always seemed to be doing. It held the heart of winter in its cold caress, a hint that it could get ever so much worse. Maxwell was glad it wasn't snowing. He still hated the snow. He still hated the cold, too, but at least if he was moving, and the temperature wasn't too low, he could bear it. But the snow, well, that made him slip and slide, and it quickly soaked through his boots. It also made it easy for the Crows to trail him.

He walked on through the night, following the ill-defined path that wove past trees, brush, thickets, and rocks. He moved steadily, though fairly slowly. What little light put out by the moon and stars was obscured by the clouds, so he proceeded cautiously. He would curse himself no end if he were to hurry too much and trip and break a bone.

He did increase his pace as he sensed that dawn was swiftly approaching. Then he slowed again when he realized he was very close to the camp. He began inching forward, and then froze as he heard a twig snap. A moment later he spotted someone moving toward him. He realized it was a warrior, apparently out to relieve himself.

Maxwell was about to let the warrior go about his business, and look for another opportunity to disrupt the overtaken camp, but then he decided that he might not get a better chance. He suddenly stepped in front of the Crow. "*Bonjour, Monsieur les Étrons*—Mister Turds," he said almost cheerfully.

The Crow stopped, and his eyes widened as he recognized Maxwell. He muttered something in his own language.

Maxwell smiled, and spit in the Indian's face. "*Le merde,*" he growled. Then he swung his rifle up in both hands and slammed it against the Crow's face. The warrior moaned and fell in a sprawling spiral. As the Crow hit the ground, Maxwell stepped up and slammed him in the head with the butt of his rifle, crushing his skull.

"Zat's one who pays ze price of provoking Jacques Maxwell," the former pirate mumbled. He slung his rifle across his back, then lifted the Crow up onto his shoulders, though it took some effort. He strode boldly right into the camp and dumped the body on the cold ground. He turned and left. In the woods, he climbed a pine and sat there waiting.

It wasn't long before the camp started awakening, and men came out of the lodges the company men had shared with their Crow women. They spotted the warrior's body and stood around, puzzled, discussing it, fear beginning to find its way into their voices.

"And 'ere is some of Asiza's medicine for you, *mes amis,*" Maxwell muttered up in his tree, calling on the voodoo spirit that dwelt in the forest and gave magical powers to men. He leveled his rifle and fired.

One of the Crows dropped, as if his legs had been chopped out from under him. Once he hit the ground, he did not move.

As Maxwell reloaded, he kept a close watch on the camp, to see what the Crows would do. One must have spotted Maxwell's powder smoke, since he pointed in that direction. A moment later, the Crows broke and ran, hurrying for their ponies.

Just before climbing down from the tree, Maxwell caught a glimpse of Dancing Water down in the camp. She seemed lost there, as if she didn't belong. Maxwell shook his head. "You're letting your imagination gone away wit' you, *mon ami*," he mumbled to himself. He decided he had seen her only as he wanted to see her, not as she was.

As he hit the ground, Maxwell spun and ran like hell. Within minutes, the Crows—angry at having lost two warriors, and deeply frightened that their war medicine had gone sour on them—were hot on his heels.

Maxwell fretted a little that the Crows were after him so quickly. He had been counting on at least a little more delay, since he was afoot and the Crows were mounted on prime, well-conditioned war ponies. He cursed once silently, but figured he had an edge in that the brush was close here along the river, and as long as he kept to it, the Crows couldn't catch him. Of course, he knew he could not stay in the brush forever. If he did, he would have to stop sooner or later, and then he would be trapped. Or else they would get too close to him, and once he did break free of the thickets, he would be easily run down.

He finally darted out of the brush, across twenty yards of open space, and then up a sharply angled cliff. As he crested the rocky outcropping, he paused just long enough to glance back. The Crows were still some distance behind him—far enough to keep him safe for at least a little longer, yet close enough for him to keep tantalizing them as he stayed just out of their reach.

He charged across the flat away from the rim of the cliff, gradually heading downward, into a small valley. He was three-quarters of the way across that, heading for another rocky bluff, when he sensed the Crows entering the valley a half a mile or so away.

Maxwell charged up the side of the other steeply sloping cliff, stopping at the top. He was wheezing from all the exertions, and his knees were shaky. He looked out across the gully, watching the Crows move slowly in his direction. He assumed they were looking for a sign that he had passed that way. He squatted, his back against a boulder, and tried to catch his breath, hoping the short rest would rebuild some of his strength. He drank deeply from the stolen wood canteen he had slung over his shoulder, glad that it wasn't summer. But the cool air was quickly getting to him, turning his sweat to ice water on him. He pushed up to his feet, and stood there for a bit, wanting to ensure that the Crows saw him. When he was certain they had, he headed on, traveling the tree- and brush-covered raggedly flat top of the mountain.

Maxwell came to another downslope leading to another small valley, and he started down it, hoping to make it across the ravine to the woods on the other side. He could do with a bit of moving through trees again, instead of up and down the sides of mountains. He slipped and slid on loose rocks, dirt, and the last of the summer-browned grass, his rifle often banging painfully against his legs and side.

He was more than halfway down the infernal slope when he stopped for a short breather. To his surprise, the Crows came riding into the valley from off to his right. Only then did he become aware that the promontory was not very long here, and the Indians had simply traveled around it in quick time.

"Merde!" he snapped, angry at himself. *"Zut! Allors!"* He was so furious that he was half convinced he should just sit right where he was and try to pick off as many of the Crows as he could before they got to him to finish him off. But even in his angry state of mind, he knew better than that. He might get one, maybe two, perhaps even three of the Crows, but certainly no more. It wasn't as if these seasoned warriors would just sit there and let themselves be shot down like sheep. Besides, there was the aftermath to consider. Even if there was only some truth to the tales he had heard about the torturous way the Indians were wont to kill people, he did not want to face that. It was one thing to go down fighting, but another entirely to be caught, trussed up like a goose for the pot, and then be tortured at the whims of the Crows.

Having caught his breath a little, Maxwell

turned and started making his way back up the slope. It was infinitely more difficult than coming down, as bad as that had been. There were not many handholds, and even fewer footholds. He would scramble ten or twelve feet up and then slide back more than half that. He made progress, but it was agonizingly slow. He paused frequently, gasping for air. Each time he did halt, feeling like a fly on the side of a cow, he checked on the Crows. They were coming steadily, but did not appear to have seen him yet.

Maxwell went back to climbing, and finally made the top again. It was all he could do to pull himself over the rim and lie there on the cold ground. His breath came in great heaves. "*Merde*," he whispered into the brown grass. "Why did I ever t'ink to do such a goddamn stupid t'ing?"

It was nearly ten minutes before he felt he could get to his feet. The Crows were at the foot of the cliff now, pointing up at him. Maxwell grabbed his crotch and shouted, "*Allez vous faire foutre, une cradingue sauvages avoir un oeil qui merde à l'autre!* Piss off, you dirty, cross-eyed savages!"

He trotted off in a roughly westward course, surprised that he had as much stamina as he did. He dodged trees and bushes, but kept close to them for the cover they provided. Eventually he realized that he was heading downward again, this time at a much gentler angle. He veered toward the edge to see if he could spot the Crows.

Spot them he did. They were riding easily up the gentle grade toward the top of the hill he was on. "*Zut! Allors!*" he growled quietly. He wanted them close to keep them interested in chasing him, but he didn't want them this close. Not this soon, anyway. He spun and ran, heading almost straight away from where the Indians were coming.

The sound of the river grew louder, which Maxwell thought might be a good thing. Perhaps he would find a cave to hide in for a while. Even if he could rest for an hour or two, he could regain a considerable amount of strength. Then he could begin the game again.

Maxwell steamed to a stop, teetering on the edge of the cliff. The Tongue River flowed by placidly—a hundred feet below. *"Heu, Monsieur Grosse Légume, t'es dans un de ces merdiers!* Well, Mister Big Shot, you're really in a fix!"

He had only one real choice, and he knew it. He moved back a few paces, then ran and jumped, pushing out as hard as he could. He hit the water hard and a little off balance, and it knocked the breath out of him. He sank like a stone for what seemed like forever before he managed to stop himself. Needing air desperately, he flapped his arms wildly and kicked his feet, forcing himself up through the water.

Two eternities later, his head popped above the surface and he drew in a long, gasping breath, then several more as he treaded water, all the while being swept downriver by the current. Finally he figured he had better get to shore. He began swimming, fighting the current as little as possible, until he at last reached the bank on the same side he had been on, but at least a mile downriver.

He crawled up the slick, muddy bank, and lay

there. Since he had been dragged so far, he figured he had some time to linger to once again try to recoup some of his vigor. He wanted nothing more than to fall asleep where he was, consequences be damned. But he would not allow himself that. Besides, he was dangerously cold and wet, and thus worried that he might fall deathly ill if he laid here too long.

He took an hour before he rose and began moving on, heading back up the river, wondering where the Crows were, and just what he was going to do next.

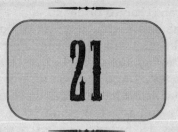

21

He found out soon enough, when he almost ran into
the Crow search party. *"Merde! Zut!"* he mumbled as
he spun and ran to his right toward a stand of trees.
"Zut! Merde! Allors!"

He could hear the Crows closing in on him as
their war cries and the pounding of their ponies
grew closer. He tried to put on another burst of
speed, but wasn't sure he actually attained it. Still,
he made it to the trees, thankful that they were
tightly packed in most places, and that there was
abundant brush woven through the trees, making it
difficult for the horses to move too fast.

Maxwell leaped over a deadfall and then
jumped, landing on his rump on the slick, steep
bank of a stream. He got to his feet in the shallow,
cold stream, splashed across it in two steps, and then
scrabbled up the equally slippery, sharply sloped
embankment. He chanced a look behind him as he
scrambled over the top of the bank.

The Crows were still in the trees, working their
way toward him as quickly as they could. Two were

on foot, running hard after him. "Damn!" he said as he turned and charged off again.

For the next two hours, Maxwell did what he could to keep ahead of the pursuing warriors—running through dense thickets or close stands of trees whenever he could. He scrambled up and down rocky, sometimes almost perpendicular, cliffs. He slid down and climbed up other slick, steep creek banks. He jumped streams, scrambled over ridges, and darted around boulders.

But he could not shake the persistent Crows. The warriors at times seemed to Maxwell to be toying with him, hanging back just enough to get him to overexert himself so that he would run himself into the ground. In his elusive lucid moments, he realized that such an idea was ridiculous. The Crows would want to catch him and get this over with so they could get back to their plunder. Besides, this chase was wearing down their horses, and from what Maxwell had heard, no Indians who prized horses as much as the Crows did would waste a valuable war horse on such a worthless—to them—target.

Having had little rest since the morning before, Maxwell knew he could not keep this up forever, so he began to set his mind to the task at hand—facing off against the horde of angry, and now bloodthirsty, he expected, Crows. He knew he had no chance of surviving any such encounter, but it would have to be done. They were going to catch him no matter what, and he wanted to take at least a few of them with him before he went under. If he kept running, he would be too weary to defend himself at all.

However, the longer he could continue to keep the Crows chasing him, the more time his companions would have to reclaim some of their property and get to safety.

It had been a hell of a long time already, and Maxwell knew he would have to give up his run soon. But the Crows made the decision for him. He wound up on an open flat after having scrambled up another slimy riverbank. He went all out, hoping to reach a small grove of trees fifty yards ahead. He made it, but he realized that several Crows were almost into the trees from the other side of the grove. He stopped and waited. He would have a minute or two, at most, to catch his breath. He was cornered, and here he would have to make a stand.

He was quite surprised when the Crows stopped on the fringes of the copse. Then one—Blue Smoke—moved toward Maxwell by himself. That was even more surprising to Maxwell. He wondered why they didn't just all charge him at the same time. But Blue Smoke was approaching, closing in on him, a shield on his left arm, a buffalo-horn war club in the right hand. He wore a fringed buckskin shirt that hung almost to his knees, and plain buckskin leggings and moccasins. The very front of his hair was cut short and stood straight up with a good coating of bear grease. The back hung loose, past his buttocks, and an eagle feather stuck straight up at the crown.

"Well, if zis is ze way it's going to be, zen so be it," Maxwell muttered in a moment of ludicrous philosophy. He didn't relish what he was about to do, but he could not afford to feel pity for any of these men or be cowardly in what needed to be done. With a shrug of slight remorse, he snatched out his pistol, palmed back the hammer, and pulled the trigger.

The snap of a misfire rattled the small copse. Birds scattered, fleeing raucously. The Crows looked startled for a moment, until they realized that his pistol had not fired.

"Zut! Allors!" Maxwell muttered. All his traipsing through streams, plus the copious sweat he had produced despite the day's cold temperatures, had dampened his powder to where it wouldn't fire. With another angry curse, he tossed the pistol away.

Blue Smoke grinned, certain now of his victory. He had had a moment's pause when he had stared at the muzzle of that big pistol pointing at his chest, but now he was serene again.

Maxwell slid out the cutlass from his pirate days, which he had carried in a sheath across his back since the day he had told his story to the others. It felt comfortable in his hand, a hefty, wide-bladed short sword that was used for hacking at an enemy, with the oddly shaped point that could be used for stabbing. He had wielded it on many a raid in the Gulf of Mexico, as well as in plenty of low dives from Galveston Island to Barataria and more.

Blue Smoke moved in, confident to the point of arrogance. He was bigger than Maxwell by several inches and perhaps twenty pounds, he was a master with the war club he carried, and he was utterly fearless. What did he have to worry about from this puny man with the odd-colored skin and the strange big knife?

Maxwell had not the time, the inclination, nor the temperament to draw this duel out. When Blue Smoke was only a few feet away, Maxwell suddenly stepped up, feinting with the cutlass toward Blue Smoke's head. The Crow raised his shield instinctively to block the thrust, leaving his midsection open. Maxwell kicked him, catching Blue Smoke's abdomen with his shin.

Blue Smoke bent double with the force of it. Maxwell took a step back, raised the cutlass, and brought it down in one swift, strong move onto the back of Blue Smoke's neck. The Crow fell, his head almost severed from his body.

Maxwell moved a little away from the body, looking from one group of Crows to the other to see what would come next. He did not gloat over his victory, nor did he defile the warrior's body any. He knew the Crows would have done so to him had he been the one to die, but he could see no reason why he should stoop to their savage ways.

Less than a minute after Blue Smoke fell, a warrior stepped away from the pack at what was for Maxwell the far end of the grove. He walked toward Maxwell, hefting a lance and a shield. Maxwell recognized him as Three Trees, a warrior renowned for his strength and tenacity. He was dressed much like Blue Smoke, although he also sported a blanket breechclout. His hair hung in two long braids on his chest.

Maxwell waited, feeling the cold wind bite through his clothes. He wiped his bloody cutlass on Blue Smoke's buckskin shirt and shoved it back into the sheath. Considering the advantage Three Trees had with the long lance, Maxwell thought he would be better off using his rifle as a defensive weapon. He pulled it over his shoulder and held it loosely in front of him at arm's length, both hands wrapped around it.

Suddenly Maxwell said quietly, "What ze 'ell." He swung the rifle around and pulled the trigger. As he suspected, it, too, had dampened powder and did not fire. But he figured it had been worth the chance.

Three Trees began his charge when the rifle misfired. Ten feet from Maxwell he stopped and hurled the lance. Surprised, Maxwell barely had time to move. The lance tore a small chunk out of his left hip.

Three Trees began running toward him again, this time with a trade tomahawk in his hand. He swung it hard and steadily at Maxwell's head. The former pirate had all he could do to keep the persistent, whirring blade from his head. Still holding his rifle crosswise, he thrust it up and out. He kept trying to hook Three Trees's tomahawk behind the blade, so he could fling it out of the warrior's hand. But the Crow was not having any of that. He just continued his relentless, bone-jarring assault.

Then Maxwell's foot slipped, and he went down hard on his back, the shock of the landing forcing him to drop his rifle. He still managed to jerk his head out of the way as Three Trees knelt and swiftly tried to split his head with the tomahawk. But Maxwell slammed an elbow into Three Trees's side, and rolled away from the Crow.

He got to his feet and before he could set

himself, Three Trees plowed into him, slamming him back up against a tree trunk. The Crow tried to kick him in the groin, but couldn't get enough leverage, so he instead jammed a forearm against Maxwell's throat and leaned his weight into it.

Choking and gasping, feeling the life being squashed out of him, Maxwell managed to raise his leg. He dropped an arm and groped around the top of the boot until he felt his dagger. He pulled it free and shoved it straight up into Three Trees's armpit.

The warrior's eyes widened with the sudden pain, then narrowed as hate built up inside him. But Maxwell wasn't interested in what the Indian was thinking or feeling. He just stabbed Three Trees in the armpit again, then in the side or abdomen, Maxwell wasn't sure, since he couldn't see.

The wounds had their effect, and Three Trees's pressure on his throat eased. Maxwell shoved his hand between himself and his adversary, and pushed Three Trees away from him. Before the Indian could regain his equilibrium, Maxwell was on him, slashing and stabbing him wherever he could reach. Within minutes, the Crow was a bloodstained, dead wretch lying on the cold ground.

"Come on, sent another one at me, you fractious piles of shit," Maxwell roared in challenge to the group of Crows. He had to wonder, however, just how many individual warriors they were going to lose this way—sending them at him one at a time— just to prove their mettle. It indeed showed their bravery, but it was foolish to continue it.

Still, another warrior moved toward him by

himself. Poor Bear was a brutish-looking and -acting warrior. He was short for a Crow, and did not have any of the Absarokas' handsomeness about him. Maxwell guessed that at least one of his parents was an outsider. He had the requisite shield and carried a war club that was reminiscent of himself—a short, stubby, unadorned haft with a broad, thick rock at the end.

Maxwell knew he would have trouble with this thug of a warrior, so he wanted an edge of some kind. He spotted his pistol and grabbed it off the ground. He wiped it quickly on his clothes to get the dirt off of it. He didn't have too much faith, but he reloaded it, hoping the gunpowder in his horn had stayed dry. He worked hastily, and was finally done.

Without delay, he turned and fired. To his great relief, the puff of smoke and the good, heavy thud told him the pistol had worked. When the wind blew away the powder smoke, though, Maxwell thought he had missed Poor Bear with the shot, which he didn't believe possible at such close range. Then he spotted the blood on Poor Bear's chest. The lead ball had hit the Crow all right, but it apparently didn't hurt the warrior much, as it didn't slow him down, or even give him pause.

"*Merde*," Maxwell said. "*Je foutre dans la merde.* I really put myself into deep shit this time." He tossed his pistol away again and turned to face this monster coming at him. He grabbed his cutlass with one hand and his dagger with the other.

There was nothing at all subtle about Poor Bear. The bullish warrior just kept on walking toward

Maxwell. When he was almost on the trader, Poor Bear swung the war club at Maxwell's head.

Had Maxwell been any slower, his head would have been splattered all over the rocks and ground. But he avoided the skull-crushing blow and stepped up, punching his dagger into Poor Bear's chest. He had aimed for the same spot where the bullet had entered, but he was off by an inch or two. There was no time to make another attempt at it, as Poor Bear was about to take another mighty swing at his head with that deadly war club.

Maxwell danced back and out of the way, keeping just out of Poor Bear's reach. But the Crow was unyielding, and kept coming at Maxwell, the brutal war club humming through the air as it sought Maxwell's fragile flesh and bones.

Maxwell was getting tired again. He had been up for more than a full day now, with the exception of a few hours' nap here and there, and the lack of sleep plus all the exertions were taking a toll on him. It also made his temper even shorter than it had been, and he was by now furious with the tenacity and singlemindedness of Poor Bear.

"Zat's it, *monsieur*," he spat at Poor Bear. "I 'ave 'ad enough of zis *merde*." He slipped under another mighty swing of the war club, rose to full height, and half turned back. He slashed down with the cutlass, catching the back of Poor Bear's wrist, nearly severing the hand from the arm. The war club fell from the useless hand.

Poor Bear, who was not the smartest of men, just stood there, looking at his hand dangling by little more than a thin strip of flesh at the bottom. It wasn't as if he were in shock from the pain, he didn't even seem to know he should be in pain. It was more a look of fascination and wonderment that this could have happened to him.

Maxwell, however, was taking no more chances. He just slid the dagger away into the boot sheath and then proceeded to hack the puzzled Poor Bear to death with the cutlass. It didn't take long.

He finally stood over the body, breathing heavily. He looked at each group of warriors at either end of the grove. He threw his head back and roared. It was not a word or phrase, just a ululating sound of pain, anger, frustration; a heartfelt bellow of victory and knowledge of impending doom; a challenge to the Crows who were still here.

As the sound faded into the chill afternoon, silence grew until it reigned over the area. Suddenly the quiet was pierced to the heart by Great Bear's war cry. Then the warriors attacked en masse, charging on foot from both ends of the copse.

Knowing that he was about to be in one hell of a fight, and certain that he would be dead soon, Maxwell moved away from the corpses that littered the area. He wanted a place where he would be able to defend himself without having to worry about tripping over bodies. He settled on a spot ten yards away that was clear of underbrush. Three tall pines grew virtually side by side, which would protect his back to some extent. He still didn't think he had much chance of withstanding the frontal assault the Crows would throw at him, but this way he should be able to take out a few more of the warriors.

He leaned back against the trees as he tried to get a breath. He held the cutlass in one hand, the retrieved dagger in the other. He had only moments to wait before the nearest group of warriors would be closing in fast on him.

22

Within moments, it seemed to Maxwell as if the Crows were coming at him from every which way, multiplying as they got near.

Determined not to sell his life cheaply, he hacked and slashed with cutlass and dagger. He kicked and punched, the weapons in his hands adding impetus to the blows; and he bit when any one of the warriors was foolish enough to get some piece of his flesh too near the almost maniacal former pirate.

Maxwell didn't know how many Crows he had wounded in some fashion, but he knew his blades were connecting with a good bit of Crow flesh and bone. Still, there seemed to be no end of warriors. In his fury, he did not feel the wounds the Indians inflicted on him. Even if he had, he would not have cared, so focused on his task was he.

He surprised the Indians when he suddenly jumped into a pile of them, knocking at least three or four down, and sprawling atop them. He scrambled up as he felt a knife or tomahawk slice down his back.

"Vous et ne pas valoir un pet de lapin un têtê de mule— You are worthless, stupid fools!" Maxwell shouted. "Come and got me, you *vieille biques*—old hags!"

Apparently a good many of the Crows understood his French—or at least they got his meaning from his expressions—for they charged at him again, swarming over him like bears on a rotted, insect-infested log. He went down, cursing and still fighting.

"Well, zis was it, *Monsieur* Jacques Maxwell," he muttered under the pile of bodies. He was happy that he was going to die bravely, and that he had nothing to be too ashamed about as he went under. He could die proudly.

He didn't know how he managed, but he squiggled his way out from under the pile until he was breathing free again. *"Sacre bleu!"* he breathed, amazed at his good fortune.

Maxwell didn't have long to enjoy it, however, since the Crows were coming at him again, their eyes reflecting their fury.

Suddenly an enraged Thornton and Lepari burst on the scene, their violence almost awesome in its intensity.

Maxwell howled as wildly as any Crow warrior, and he waded back into the battle.

The sudden assault from a new and unexpected source—plus Maxwell's renewed fury—shocked and demoralized the Crows. Feeling that their medicine had been broken, they scattered and fled, scooping up their dead and wounded as they melted into the trees, heading for their ponies.

Then the three companions were standing alone,

with the wind and their labored breathing the only sounds.

"Where did you boys came from, eh?" Maxwell wheezed as he watched the Crows galloping off.

"Figured you could use a mite of help, ol' friend," Thornton said with a grin.

"Well, *mes amis*, you figured right. *Mais oui*. But I t'ink you could 'ave figured it a little sooner, *ça va?*"

"Damn, if that don't beat all, Pete," Thornton said. "We save this crusty ol' fart's festerin' hide, and all he can do is complain that we ain't fast enough. Well, the hell with you, mister. The next time, we won't come save your ass a'tall." He was grinning all the while he was speaking.

"If I 'ave to rely on ze likes of you two, *mes amis*, zen I am in big trouble, *comprendez?*"

"Go to hell, you ol' windbag."

"We better hurry, boys," Lepari said, chewing his nails again now that his weapons had been put away. "Them Crows might be headin' back toward the others, and they ain't happy, I expect."

"Ze others?" Maxwell asked sharply, squinting with one eye at Lepari. "Where are zey?"

"Back in our original camp," Thornton answered. "The one that was took over by those savages."

"Is it far?" Maxwell asked, suspicious and wary, though he didn't know why.

"Ain't but a couple of miles," Lepari noted. "For all the runnin' you did, you never got very far."

"*Zut! Allors!*" Maxwell groused. He started walking off. "Well, zen, *mes amis*, let's go. *Allons.*" Suddenly he stopped. "You 'ave 'orses?" he asked.

"Hell, yes," Thornton said, sounding almost

offended. "You think we enjoy walkin' around these parts as much as you do?"

"*Aiie*," Maxwell snapped. "But I 'ave not'ing to ride."

"Hell, you can ride double with one of us if we can't catch one of those Crows' ponies loiterin' about," Lepari said matter-of-factly.

Maxwell nodded. "*Allons, mes amis.*"

"What about your wounds, Jacques?" Thornton asked. He had just seen the big bloody rip through Maxwell's shirt and skin.

"What about zem, *mon ami?*" Maxwell asked, his face suddenly gone hard again.

"Don't you need to care for them?"

"*Mais oui.* But later will be time enough. We must get back to ze others, *n'est-ce pas?*"

"Reckon so," Thornton said. Then he grinned again. "If you think you can make it."

Maxwell's look shook Thornton momentarily. It was an expression of utter disdain and fierce pride.

"Sorry," Thornton mumbled.

It took less than five minutes for Lepari and Thornton, once they were mounted, to coax one of the Crow ponies into their possession. Moments later, Maxwell, his weapons retrieved and placed back where they should be, pulled himself up onto the unfamiliar horse. He wondered if he would be able to ride the thing for any length of time. He had enough trouble riding with one of their crude saddles; doing so bareback might be a real adventure. The horse, however, had an easy gait, and Maxwell soon found there was no reason for concern.

They wasted no time heading for the old camp.

They simply got the horses moving fast and kept up that pace. They took a direct route for the most part, veering only when they had to go around a hill or some other obstruction that was too big or difficult to go over. Within a half hour, they were slowing their horses, the camp in view. They came almost to a walk, wanting to make sure the Crows who had attacked Maxwell had not returned and retaken the camp.

Their friends must have sensed them coming, for they soon came out of the lodges and waited.

"Ze women, zey are still 'ere?" Maxwell suddenly asked, surprised.

"Most of 'em," Lepari said.

"But . . ."

"We'll explain it all later."

Before the men gathered in Maxwell's lodge, however, Lepari made sure that Dancing Water treated Maxwell's back wound, as well as the numerous other wounds, big and small, he had received in his battle with the Crows that day.

Soon after, they were sitting in Maxwell's old lodge. Dancing Water was there, as were Lodge Fire, Falls Plenty, and Sun Woman. Maxwell had also seen Yellow Crow, Singing Flower, and Leaping Fox when he had ridden into the camp, but they were not in the lodge.

"So, tell me what 'appened, *mes amis*," Maxwell said. He nodded gratefully but still warily at Dancing Water when she handed him a mug of coffee and a bowl of elk stew.

The others looked around, waiting for someone to say something, though no one appeared willing. Finally, all the other men were staring at Lepari, so

Maxwell turned his gaze to him, too. "Well, *mon ami?*" Maxwell asked.

"Well, Jacques," Lepari started. He seemed uncomfortable, but determined to live up to the task that had been presented him. "We did what you said, and waited at that other place a spell. Not as long as some of us thought prudent," he added, looking pointedly at Beecher. "Anyway, when we got here, most of the Crows were gone, chasin' off after you. But a few Crows were left behind to watch over all our plunder, as you figured they'd do. Anyway, we was fit to be tied by then, I'll tell you. Hungry, cold, tired, and just plain ol' goddamn angry. So . . . "

"So," Beecher tossed in boastfully, "we kicked their asses, but good. Counted coup on 'em, as they're so fond of sayin' they do. Killed ever' last one of them stinkin' savages."

"Was zat ze way of it, Pierre?" Maxwell asked Lepari.

"Pretty much. There wasn't but four of 'em, and they weren't payin' too much attention to things, so it wasn't as hard as some might want you to believe." He grinned at Beecher.

"And ze women?" Maxwell asked. He was still highly suspicious of them.

"Well, sir, they caused us some consternation tryin' to figure out what to do about 'em. We knew Yellow Crow was no good, since she'd gone to fetch Great Bear and the others. So we was mighty suspicious of the others, too."

"Good t'inking, *mon ami*," Maxwell said seriously.

Lepari shrugged. "We also saw Singin' Flower consortin' with one of the Crows just before we attacked the camp. I figured Lucius might give us some trouble when we rounded her up and stuck her with Yellow Crow, but that boy was nigh on to killin' her before me and Milt stopped him."

"What about ze others?"

Lepari could not suppress a snort. "Well, for some goddamn reason, Sun Woman really took a shine to Henry. Right from the beginnin'. As soon as we were done dispatchin' those Crows, Sun Woman was weepin' in Henry's arms like she was his long-lost love or somethin'."

Maxwell glanced over at Thornton, who was red as a beet. He also stole a glance at Sun Woman, who was clearly embarrassed, but equally as proud.

"Anyway, she 'fessed up to him and the rest of us about the whole thing."

"Great Bear planned something like zis all along, eh?" Maxwell asked.

"How'd you know?"

"Didn't know for sure, but I t'ought it likely. It was my suspicious nature, I t'ink, zat made me t'ink zat way."

"Well, it was a plot, for certain. At first, the women were supposed to keep us happy and stupid. Then, when spring came, the Crows were gonna trade with us like everything was right. Then, once we rode out of the village, they were gonna kill us and take all their furs back, plus the horses and everythin' else and leave us out here to feed the coyotes and buzzards."

"Fine bunch of fellers," Richwine rumbled.

"Oui," Maxwell said absentmindedly. There was something here that did not add up.

"Anyway," Lepari continued, "once we determined to leave the village right away, they just concocted a plot based on the old one but with some new things added. The women were to come with us so we wouldn't be suspicious, but they were to mark the trail as we rode. That way Great Bear and the warriors could follow us. When we made our camp here, Yellow Crow was chosen to be the one to go out and tell Great Bear where we were."

"Then George found out she was gone and went after her," Nordgren said bitterly. "And, of course, he ran into that whole passel of Crows."

Maxwell nodded, still troubled by something. "What about Leaping Fox?" he asked.

"She was involved in the plot," Richwine rumbled. Leaping Fox was the woman with whom he had been paired, and he did not like the fact that she had betrayed him and the others.

Maxwell nodded again. "It wasn't your fault, *mon ami*." Suddenly something clicked, and he knew what was troubling him. "Why would ze Crows do zat, zough?" he asked, almost as if musing aloud. "Zey 'ave always been friendly to ze traders and especially *Monsieur* Lisa's company, from all we 'eard."

The men sat there, looking baffled. It had never occurred to them that such action by the Crows was out of character.

"Husband," Dancing Water said contritely in her heavily accented English, "me speak?"

A surprised Maxwell nodded.

"Great Bear very angry at Trading Chief," Dancing Water said hesitantly. She knew her English was not very good, and she wanted to make sure she did not misspeak. "Two summers ago, Trading Chief's men came to village. They promise many things. But when spring came, they give firewater to the men and pay nothing for furs. And they take two women who not want to go. They . . . "

Maxwell held up his hand. "That's enough, woman," he said. He looked around the circle of men. "Looks like zese Crows 'ad zeir reasons for wanting us dead, eh, *mes amis?*"

"Still don't mean I got to like the bastards," Beecher said, still angry, hurt, and even somewhat ashamed.

"*Oui*, zat is so. But now at least we understand zem a little, eh? Zey could not trust us. We could not trust zem, *voila!* We 'ave big trouble."

"You're mighty understandin' about all this, Jacques," Beecher said. "Why? Because your woman says she wasn't a traitor like Singin' Flower was? How do you know for sure?"

"Would you like me to answer one of zose questions or all of zem at ze same time?" Maxwell responded, his voice hard. "I am understanding because I 'ave met many men in my life. Some good, some bad. I even know some good white men. 'Ard to t'ink, maybe, but it's true. I 'ave met some very evil men *aussi*. Men who are like Perfect Duffant—ze devil 'imself—whose evil you can't even begun to understood. More evil zan zese Crows could ever be. But more, *mon ami*, zese men 'ad a reason for what zey did, *ça va?* Zey did not do zis just to be mean, but to pay back some of ze wrong done to zem. Just like we pay zem back for ze bad t'ings zey done to us."

Maxwell paused and finished his coffee. He was

finally feeling truly warm after having been cold for so long. "As for Dancing Water," he shrugged. "Maybe I do 'ave a soft 'ead, eh? I t'ink she is not a traitor no more. What you t'ink?"

"I think I'm a goddamn fool half the time, Jacques," Beecher said ruefully. "I'm jist angry as hell 'cause it was my woman turned out to be one of the betrayers. Damn, if that don't beat all."

"Yours wasn't the only one turned against us, Lucius," Richwine said sadly. He was a big man, tough and hard, but as honest as could be. He asked few things of life, and thought he had found one of them in Leaping Fox. But his dreams had been dashed.

They sat in relative silence, slurping stew or coffee, lighting pipes, or just sitting with eyes closed, recalling all that had gone on in the past couple of days. It had been more than most of them had bargained for when they set out on this expedition, their minds dimmed then by all the glory that they were about to reap. None had thought much of the gut-wrenching, ball-twisting, sweat-producing fear; or the fact that they would have to kill another human being; nor could they have foreseen the blood and bits of flesh that splattered them in the midst of fighting, or the fact of seeing the light go out for the last time in another man's face.

Now they had seen it all, and they were not sure they had liked it one bit, though all that gloom was softened considerably by the good things—the taste of savory buffalo meat, of a well-cooked stew, the pleasures of a Crow woman in the robes, the sense of victory, the knowledge that one had survived another day when others had not.

23

The next morning, Maxwell and his men headed off, pushed by the new snowfall. Winter was coming fast, and the group had to find someplace to spend the cold months.

"Why don't we jist stay here?" Beecher had asked late the night before, as the men discussed their immediate future.

Lepari snorted. "Sure, Lucius. And why don't we just go and plunk our carcasses right outside Great Bear's village."

"What the hell's that supposed to mean?" Beecher snapped. He was tired and just wanted some sleep before these momentous decisions were made. And if they were to be made then, he wanted them over and done with as soon as possible.

"It means, you dumb fart," Thornton said evenly, "that this place is a mite close to Great Bear's village to be comfortable. Knowin' how notional those savages can be, there ain't no tellin' but what Great Bear might git back his courage and come a-lookin' for us again."

"All right, dammit," Beecher said in annoyance, hating to be made out a fool like this. "So where do we go?"

Everyone looked at Maxwell, who shrugged. "I don' know where to gone. I don' know zis country any better zan you. But Pierre is right—we can't stay 'ere."

"What do you suggest we do, Jacques?" Thornton asked.

"Follow ze Tongue Rivair across ze mountains, I suppose. Trade, if we can, trap when we can't, until we find a place to spend ze wintair."

"Brilliant plan, Jacques," Beecher snapped.

"Do you 'ave a bettair one, *mon ami?*" Maxwell responded, unfazed.

"No," Beecher admitted.

"Zen zat's what we'll do," Maxwell said with finality. "Does anyone else have anyt'ing to say?" He looked from one man to another.

"What about the women?" Lepari suddenly asked.

"What about zem?"

"You sure we can trust 'em, Jacques? After what was already done."

"Sun Woman didn't have much of a part in all that," Thornton said. He liked his woman quite a lot, and was not thrilled with the idea of not having her around.

Maxwell thought about it for a while. It was true that, except for Singing Flower and Leaping Fox, the women seemed to have little connection with Great Bear's plot—or else they were just professing to be contrite. Still, it would be hard to fully trust any of them. "Let me t'ink on it, *mes amis*. I'll tell you my decision in ze morning, before we leave 'ere."

The others weren't entirely happy with that, but they were all tired and hoped to get to sleep. And some still had their women, so they wanted to enjoy their delights at least once more. All filed out, heading for their own lodges.

Maxwell sat there long after the others were gone. He enjoyed having Dancing Water around, but there was still the little matter of not knowing exactly how much she was involved in Great Bear's plans for his men. He considered taking all the women with them, but he wasn't sure that would be wise.

He also pondered taking all but Singing Flower and Leaping Fox. That appealed to him. It would keep him and most of the others in female companionship. It also might make their entry into other Indian villages, particularly Crow ones, easier. And unless they traveled a long, long way, they would have to deal with Crows. If Dancing Water's story about Great Bear's anger at Manuel Lisa's men was true, the trouble with the Crows would likely be restricted to this one band. The other Crow villages might be more welcoming to Maxwell and his men if they were escorted by Crow women. On the other hand, the women might be hiding feelings of anger, and make up stories about the men, thus bringing the wrath of another band of Crows down on them.

When it was all considered, the choice was obvious to Maxwell. He could not take the chance of having the women betray them again. They may have no intention of doing so, he knew, but the risk was too great. He sighed, looking at Dancing Water. He would have been happy with her, had events been different. He knocked the ashes out of his pipe and rose. "Come to ze robes, woman," he said quietly.

The men were, for the most part, not pleased with Maxwell's decision when he told them in the morning. But they were also fatalistic about it. They understood his reasoning when he explained it to them, and none had any hankering to die just to continue enjoying the pleasures of a particular woman.

Of the group, only Beecher was glad at the outcome. Since Singing Flower had been the second-biggest traitor among the women, and he would not have her now anyway, he was secretly happy that no one else would have a woman for the winter either.

Once the men had held their meeting—out in the open, without the women around—each man went to tell his woman that she would not be coming along.

Maxwell explained it to Dancing Water, who stared at him with icy eyes. He was not sure if Dancing Water was so cold to him because she truly cared for him or because she saw her plans foiled again. He almost changed his mind when she coldly told him that she was in no way involved in any new plot against him and the others, but he remained stolid.

As Dancing Water continued to argue with him,

Maxwell grew weary of it. He wanted to be away from here as soon as possible. He was concerned that Great Bear's Crows would return at any time to avenge their humiliation. "Zat is enough!" he finally said sharply. "If you keep up zis arguing, I won't even gave you and ze other women 'orses to get back to ze village, *ça va?*"

"You were gonna give horses?" Dancing Water asked, surprised.

"*Oui.*"

"All of us?"

"*Non.* Singing Flower and Leaping Fox will 'ave to walk. Or zey can ride double wit' you and ze others, if you want zat. But zey don' deserve any 'orses after what zey did to us, *n'est-ce pas?*"

Dancing Water nodded. She could see in Maxwell's black face that he was not about to give up anything else, and that to argue any more would mean losing the horses. She would have to settle for that. She would miss him, though. He would not believe her if she told him that, and she could not blame him. But she had come to care for Maxwell in the short time they had been together. He was as brave as any Crow warrior she knew, and he had a good heart. She wished now that she had never let Great Bear talk her into betraying this man. It had not seemed so devious at first. After all, at the time, she barely knew Maxwell, and so she did not care all that much what happened to him. But as she saw his strength and courage, his generosity and his leadership, her outlook had changed.

Dancing Water sighed as she packed her things. It was too late for any of that now. She could always hope that one day he would come back, though she knew in her heart that such a thing was not likely. Not after the trouble between Maxwell's men and Great Bear's warriors. She was glad that Maxwell had left the lodge. That way he would not have to see the tears that leaked from her expressive brown eyes.

Outside, Maxwell could hear Sun Woman screeching at Thornton, and he almost smiled. But not quite. He was taken with Dancing Water, and wished things had turned out differently. So he could not be too amused by another woman giving her man a hard time about being sent away. However, he did hope that Thornton would end the quarreling soon, since there was plenty of work to be done before they could depart.

He went to help load their supplies and goods. Richwine and Beecher, not having any women to break the bad news to, were already hard at work. It helped them keep their minds off of what was going on around them, Maxwell suspected. Nordgren was also there, still limping from the wound he had suffered.

"You 'ave any trouble telling Falls Plenty?" Maxwell asked, as he threw himself into the work.

"No," Nordgren said with a shrug. "I yoost told her I vas going and dot she was going back to her village. Dot vas dot." He grinned a little. "But I don't think Henry is finding it so easy to do, yah?"

Maxwell figured he could allow a small smile at that. "I'd say not, *mon ami*. She is giving zat boy an 'ard time."

Before long, though, all the men were working at packing goods and loading and saddling horses. Finally they were finished. Maxwell turned and saw that all the lodges but his had been taken down. "What ze 'ell?" he wondered aloud. He could see Dancing Water walking toward him, and he moved to meet her. "Why isn't ze lodge down, woman?" he asked.

"The men must eat before they go. Yes. So we leave our . . . my . . . lodge up. We eat there." She looked up at him, her eyes questioning whether that was acceptable.

"*Bon*," Maxwell said with a strong nod. "It's a good idea, Dancing Water. *Mais oui. Merci beaucoup*."

Dancing Water tried to hide the joy that rose up inside her. She thought she managed well.

Minutes later, they were all crammed in the one big lodge, the men slurping down bowls of stewed meat. They were all hungry from their labors, and knew they faced a long, hard ride in the cold and snow, so they planned to fill themselves up with good, hot food.

Afterward, while the other women started taking the tipi down, and the men went to get the horses, Maxwell and Dancing Water stood in the middle of the camp. "Zat was a good t'ing you did, Dancing Water," Maxwell said, smiling down at her.

"You deserve."

"Maybe we do, but maybe not." He shrugged. "No matter." He paused. "You'll be careful on ze way back to ze village, eh?"

Dancing Water nodded, not trusting herself to talk.

"I don't like doing zis, you know, *ma femme*."

Dancing Water nodded again.

"But it 'as to be," Maxwell added lamely. He pulled her to him and held her close. "*Au 'voir*, Dancing Water." Maxwell abruptly pulled himself away from the woman and headed toward his horse. He did not look back as he mounted the animal and led the way out of the camp. He blamed the sudden wetness on his face on the snow that had begun to fall.

Without saying anything about their troubles with Great Bear's band, the small group traded with several other villages of Crows. While they were friendly, and offered fair trades with the Indians for their furs, the company men were always wary and they never stayed too close or too long with any one band.

However, they took every opportunity they could to bed some of the attractive Crow women along the way. Maxwell wondered about the others, but he knew that he was trying to get over Dancing Water. Not a day went by that he didn't regret not having brought her along. He berated himself silently for mistrusting her. But in his mind, he knew he had done the right thing, as least as far as his and his men's survival was concerned, as well as the company's profits. He had promised to give his all for the company, and that's what he was trying to do. Still, his heart ached, and only the transient comfort of a Crow woman's charms could soothe his aching spirit, and then just temporarily.

Finally the men found a spot along the Bighorn River to winter up. By the time they had constructed some rude shelters for themselves and storage for their furs and trade goods, the winter was hard on them. It snowed regularly, and the wind howled like wretched banshees around them. The temperature was so cold, it snapped tree branches with loud cracking sounds that sounded like gunshots to the jumpy mountaineers, though they knew better.

Still suspicious, the men kept a constant watch over their camp, worried that some band of Crows—or even some other Indians—would attack. But the winter was uneventful, even boring to the men. And, though they remained anxious throughout the cold months, they relaxed as the weeks passed.

As the spring approached, their anxiety found renewal. They knew that if any Indians were going to attack, they would do it in the spring, once the bands had had their big hunt.

Still, the men were happy when winter began to loosen its grip. They were tired of being holed up, of having to kick snow off the roofs of their crude buildings, of having to make sure the horses had something to eat, of making sure they had something to eat. And they were tired of being with each other, without any women around.

So it was with considerable joy that they finally broke camp and began their long, slow trek back to the fort. The men trapped when and where they could, though they were counting on the Crows for most of the plews they took.

They stopped to trade whenever they came upon a Crow village. Again, they were constantly on the alert, but they had no real trouble. The Crows seemed glad to see them for the most part, and were happy to trade their furs for the wonders the white men had packed along. Maxwell's men, in turn, were happy with the furs they traded for, and even more joyous at being able to spend a night or two with a woman.

With spring well on its way, they finally reached the fort, where they told their story—with considerable exaggeration about their bravery. And they learned what happened to the other small brigades that had gone out. Some of them had fared well, some poorly. None brought in as many pelts as Maxwell's crew, however.

"Mister Lisa will be mighty pleased when he sees what you and your boys have done, Jacques," Giles Elgood said. "He appreciates men who can accomplish a lot."

Maxwell shrugged. "I was 'ired to do a job, and I did ze best I could wit' it, *Monsieur le Capitaine*," he said. "Ze others feel ze same."

"I'm glad to hear that, Jacques," the expedition leader said. He paused, then added, "And because of the fine job you and your men did, I'd like to offer you the post of second in command."

"*Merci, Monsieur le Capitaine*," Maxwell said, "but I don' t'ink I wan' dat."

"What're you going to do?" Elgood asked, surprised.

"I don't knew what. But zere's a lot of land to was seen and squaws to took to ze robes and beaver to been trapped. And I prefer to done it by myself, not wit' a company."

"You're still under contract, Jacques. You know that," Elgood said.

"Try 'olding me to it," Maxwell challenged, but he smiled a little.

The fort grew tense, the men not wanting to take sides. Just about all of them liked Maxwell, but as the expedition leader, Elgood would be paying their wages.

"Why don't you let Jacques leave with jist his own plunder and enough food and supplies to last him a few weeks?" Beecher suddenly chimed in. "In return, you'd not have to pay him."

"Just void our contract?" Elgood asked, intrigued by the notion. He knew he could not hold on to Maxwell if the former pirate decided to just walk out.

"Yep," Beecher said with a nod.

"That suit you, Jacques?" Elgood asked, looking at Maxwell.

"*Oui*," Maxwell said after only a moment's thought.

"Then it's done," Elgood said with some sadness. He liked Maxwell and would hate to see him go. "Any idea where you might be headin'?" he asked.

Maxwell shrugged. "Maybe I'll 'ead to Spanish country. But maybe not." He had a sudden vision of Dancing Water, and wondered if she was safe in Great Bear's village. He considered the possibility of going to get her.

"Well, Jacques, I wish you luck," Elgood said. The two shook hands. "And don't you forget, my friend, that if you're lookin' for work, come see me. There'll always be somethin' for you."

"*Merci beaucoup, Monsieur le Capitaine,*" Maxwell said, and went off to pack his few supplies.

While he was doing so, Thornton, Lepari, and Beecher strolled up. "Me, Pete, and Lucius want to come with you," Thornton said flatly.

"I didn't want you to do zat, *mes amis.*"

"You owe us," Beecher said evenly. "It was me, after all, who come up with the idea that got you your freedom here. And it was Henry and Pete who saved your ass back during that fight with the Crows."

"Guess you was right, maybe," Maxwell reluctantly said. He really did prefer to trap and travel alone, especially if he was going to go find Dancing Water, which was fast becoming his plan. But his three friends had matured considerably and he figured they would be worthwhile companions. And he knew it would be far safer to travel with this small group of men who knew each other and liked each other, who would be willing to protect each other during hard times.

Still, one problem remained, one that might still have him riding out solo. "You boys will 'ave to made your own deal wit' *Monsieur le Capitaine* to got out of your contracts."

"Already did," Beecher replied with a wide grin.

"Zen got packing, *mes amis*, and be quick about it," Maxwell said. He smiled as the three younger men ran off. He looked off to the west, seeing a lodge standing there, and Dancing Water waiting for him. "*Oui*, Jacques, zat is ze way to gone," he said quietly.

JOHN LEGG is a full-time writer and newspaper editor who lives in Arizona with his family.

If you would like to be placed on John Legg's mailing list, in order to receive periodic newsletters and updates on new books, please send a postcard to:

John Legg
P.O. Box 39032
Phoenix, AZ 85069

Please note on the postcard if you would like to receive a current list of Mr. Legg's books.

Thank you for your interest. Happy reading!